THE WONDERFUL FLIGHT
TO THE MUSHROOM PLANET

BOOKS BY ELEANOR CAMERON

The Green and Burning Tree

A Room Made of Windows

The Terrible Churnadryne

THE MUSHROOM PLANET SERIES

The Wonderful Flight to the Mushroom Planet

Stowaway to the Mushroom Planet

Mr. Bass's Planetoid

A Mystery for Mr. Bass

Time and Mr. Bass

The Wonderful Flight
to the Mushroom Planet

by ELEANOR CAMERON

Little, Brown and Company
Boston • New York • Toronto • London

LIBRARY OF CONGRESS CATALOG CARD NUMBER 54-8310

ISBN: 0-316-12537-7 (HC)
ISBN: 0-316-12540-7 (PBK)

HC: 30   29   28   27   26   25
PB: 10   9   8

MV=NY

*Published simultaneously in Canada
by Little, Brown & Company (Canada) Limited*

PRINTED IN THE UNITED STATES OF AMERICA

To my son, the real David, who asked for this book and who edited it with a stern black pencil — and to Ian, who whispered in Mr. Bass's ear the secret of the marvelous stroboscopic polaroid filter — with my love and my thanks.

Contents

PART ONE

Mr. Bass

CHAPTER 1

A Little Planet
Just My Size

ONE NIGHT after dinner when David was reading *Doctor Dolittle in the Moon,* and his father was reading the newspaper, and his mother was darning socks, his father suddenly exclaimed:

"Well, now, *that's* very odd!"

"What's odd?" David and his mother both asked at once.

"Why," said his father, "this notice in the paper."

David went over to look, and there, down at the very bottom corner of the next to the last page of the newspaper, were a few lines of print. But though the rest of the newspaper was printed in black, this little notice was in green. Here is what it said:

WANTED: A small space ship about eight feet long, built by a boy, or by two boys, between

3

the ages of eight and eleven. The ship should be sturdy and well made, and should be of materials found at hand. Nothing need be bought. No adult should be consulted as to its plan or method of construction. An adventure and a chance to do a good deed await the boys who build the best space ship. Please bring your ship *as soon as possible* to Mr. Tyco M. Bass, 5 Thallo Street, Pacific Grove, California.

Well, a notice like that sprung suddenly on any boy, just because of its general air of mystery and urgency, would be enough to start him simmering. But for David it was stupendous!

Regularly, every night after he got into bed and the light was turned out, he took off in his own imaginary space ship. Making peculiar, jagged noises like "rht-tttttt-chsssssssss" or "r-r-r-r-r-r-ram-am-ama-am-BOOM!" he'd poise for a second on the window sill. And then — with a horrible roar and a blinding burst of light — he'd streak off smooth and powerful and free as a bullet into the far, far reaches of the sky. He'd flash past Mars and Jupiter, turn, take a couple of whirls around the dead and glowing moon (right around the frozen, dark side nobody else has ever seen) and be back again in a wink.

But it was all imagination. He could stare as

4

much as he liked at his big map of the solar system tacked up on the wall, but he was still exactly where he had been in the first place.

So you can understand what the sight of that little green notice in the paper did to him, how it set him vibrating like a harp in the wind. *Build a real space ship all his own.* Why, he'd never thought of that! And yet, why not? And then, after that —

"But it's a joke," said Dr. Topman firmly, after a moment or two in which he must have been cogitating. "I'll bet you anything it's just some sort of joke — and a pretty poor one at that."

"Oh, but Father, it can't be! *Why* would it be a joke?"

"The notice is in green," said his mother, smiling to herself. "I wonder what Mr. Bass is like." Then she bit off her thread and held up a sock to the lamp to be sure she'd done a good job.

"Well, by George," said Dr. Topman, "I'll bet Mr. Bass has vanished by now. Because there *is* no such street as Thallo Street in this town. After all the calls I've made, I think I ought to know. Sounds made up to me."

An adventure and a chance to do a good deed await the one who builds the finest ship!

"Oh, Father," burst out David, "what *kind* of an adventure, do you suppose?"

But Dr. Topman only muttered to himself something about its being a crime to lead children on like that, and about there being a catch to it somewhere. Then he tossed aside the page containing the mysterious little notice and buried himself in the rest of the paper.

David looked at his mother. She winked at him and held out her scissors, and in a minute David had the notice all cut out and neatly folded up in his pocket.

Tomorrow morning, he said to himself, he'd begin working on his design for the ship — or he'd begin hunting around to see how much material he could find to build it. And maybe Chuck Masterson could dig out a lot of old boards and stuff nobody wanted any more over in his grandfather's boathouse. But then all at once he thought: Why not begin drawing the plans right away? So he got some paper and a pencil and started to work.

"Father!" exclaimed David as he drew his first lines.

"Yes, David," answered his father patiently, putting down his newspaper.

6

"What would the earth look like from way out in the sky, thousands of miles away?"

"We-e-ll," replied Dr. Topman, seeming to consider, "I can't imagine. But one thing I know, all around us stretches the absolute black of space, even with the sun burning and flaming away out there like a huge furnace — space that is almost empty inside and around our solar system, but that beyond is crowded with stars even in the daytime. Because, as a matter of fact, you see, there *is* no daytime out there — no wind, no sound, nothing but blackness and the eternal movements of those little points of light."

No daytime, no wind, no sound, nothing but blackness!

"But Father, *why* is there no daytime there, even if the sun is shining?"

"Because there is nothing out there to *reflect* the sun's light, David. Atmosphere, made up of gases, surrounds our earth, so that whatever part of the earth the sun is shining on has light — the atmosphere reflects it. The atmosphere carries sound, causes the winds. But not out in space. And if you were thousands of miles away and looking at the earth," continued Dr. Topman, "you would see both day and night from there

7

at once, if the sun were in the right position."

David, with his tongue in the corner of his mouth, held his breath while he drew an almost perfect curve.

"Do you suppose I'll ever be a space man, Father?" he asked longingly.

"Shouldn't be at all surprised," answered his father in a perfectly matter-of-fact way. "Shouldn't be at all surprised. But *I'll* never be — all that's beyond my time. Besides, I like my own home and the view of the bay out our back windows. Catch me whizzing around through space — not on your life!"

By bedtime, half an hour later, David had a most beautiful diagram of his space ship all finished.

The ship was long and smooth and cigar-shaped, with a slender pointed nose. It had one big window at the front. Just back of the window there was a door which could be bolted tight. The ship had no wings, but it had four broad blades for a tail, set at right angles to one another around the rocket exhaust. They were level at the ends so that the space ship could sit upended on them quite firmly, and they were curved on the inside edges where they extended below the exhaust. There was a cross-section drawing of the ship, so that you could see its interior, and a rear-view, a side-view, and a front-view drawing.

Tomorrow was Tuesday, the second day of Easter vacation. He and Chuck would have to work fast. They would have to keep their plans secret, and the building of the space ship hidden — maybe down in that cave on Cap'n Tom's beach — so no other fellows could see what they were doing and steal their ideas. And they wouldn't even tell Cap'n Tom, who was Chuck's grandpop, because Cap'n Tom would want to help build.

Now David wandered away to his own room and slowly and thoughtfully began to get undressed. Finally, quite a bit later, and still thinking hard about frameworks and air pressure and velocity and all that, he climbed into bed and curled into a ball. But when his father and mother came in to say good night and turn out the light, he sat up again.

"You know what?" he said, looking up at the moon that was sending a pale beam through his window.

"What, David?" asked his father and mother,

stopping to listen.

"I'd like to find a little planet just my size — not a big one like the earth that takes months and months to get around, but a nice *little* one that you could explore in a day or two."

"But I'm afraid that's not possible, David," said Dr. Topman, smiling down at him, "not for ten or twenty years yet, or maybe even fifty. Might be something to look forward to, though."

"Perhaps you'll find it in your dreams, David," said his mother hopefully.

"But I don't *want* to find it in my dreams," said David impatiently. "That wouldn't do at all. I don't *want* it to be a dream. I want it to be *real!*"

CHAPTER 2

At 5 Thallo Street

THROUGH the trees shone a soft, spreading light. It came from the window of Mr. Bass's cellar, and if you had peeked in, you would have seen a little old man bending over an enormous ledger. The light shining down on him was curious. It was bright and yet cool; it was gentle and yet penetrating. It had the silvery restfulness of moonlight combined with the clarity of sunlight. Mr. Bass had invented it, and had done all the wiring and the stringing up of those glowing bubbles of glass himself. But he couldn't, for the life of him, have told you *how* he had invented it.

"Fifteen and ten are twenty-five —" he muttered to himself.

He was seated on a very high stool at his workbench, and he was surrounded by such a clutter of screws and nails and wires and batteries and bits of twine and bottles of green and yellow **and**

11

raspberry colored fluids as you never saw. Behind him, piled up on the floor, were his empty mushroom boxes.

"— and six are thirty-two — no, thirty-one," said Mr. Bass, licking the end of his pencil and writing down thirty-one. Then he did some more adding and subtracting. "Five dollars and ninety-two cents," he announced finally. "But really, I don't know why I bothered. For I have a suspicion I shall have no time to spend it. However," and he sighed, "it would have been a pity to waste all those nice mushrooms." Then he turned and surveyed the rest of his cellar. "More pushing up, too. Dear me, what's to become of them? Ah, well, there's no use worrying about that now."

He put the ledger away in a drawer, stuck the pencil behind his ear, and hopped down off the stool.

"Rocket motor," he said to himself, as if he were beginning to check off items on a list in his mind. And he looked over to where a large, shining, complicated contraption rested on a broad shelf. "Fuel," he muttered, frowning and pursing his lips. Then he tapped the side of his nose and went over to a large, battered metal container which

12

looked like an old milk can. He lifted the lid and sniffed. "Hee-hee!" he chuckled. "And now for the final touch. Just those four drops of atomic tritetramethylbenzacarbonethylene." He skipped over to his bench and quickly chose a bottle, then — plop! plop! plop! plop! "Whe-e-e-e!" cried little Mr. Bass, rubbing his hands in delight. "*That'll* fix it! Blow a mountain to smithereens, that would! *Ten* mountains!" Then he printed a label which said:

FUEL FOR SPACE SHIP

and stuck it on the side of the can and put the lid back on again.

Next he went over to a big wooden vat, lifted the lid, and peered in. Then he got a huge wooden spoon and began stirring and stirring, occasionally lifting the spoon so that he could examine the smooth, clear, gluey substance that dripped from it. He seemed tremendously pleased. "Beautiful consistency," he murmured, "simply beautiful. Couldn't be better. Now — if *only* the boy doesn't take too long with his space ship. A week would see this stuff ruined. Of course, I could add a little — tarnation! What was it now? Oh well, doesn't matter — doesn't matter."

Now he popped the lid on again, leaned the spoon on a clean piece of paper against the wall, and printed another label. This time it said:

FLUID RESINOID SILICON (WITH OTHER INGREDIENTS)

FOR TREATMENT OF EXTERIOR OF SPACE SHIP

and when it was finished he pasted it onto the vat. "Never can tell," he murmured. "I just might have to leave before I can complete my mission — however, I must simply trust —"

Then he gave a last look around, turned out the light, went outside and closed the door and scurried round to the front of the house. A minute or so later he was up on the second story seated on another high stool. But this time, instead of making labels or adding and subtracting into a ledger, he was squinting through a large telescope.

"Yes," he murmured to himself, "I must have been right." Then he opened a notebook which he had by him and which was titled, in his very peculiar handwriting, *A Few Facts Concerning the Hitherto Undiscovered Satellite, Basidium-X.* He opened the notebook to a page covered with figures, and his finger went down the columns. "Diameter — thirty-five miles. Yes, yes, there's no way out of it. And yet, *if* the diameter is so small,

14

how in thunderation has it managed to hang onto its atmosphere? The smaller the planet, the less gravity it has, and therefore the less atmosphere. A puzzle! A most extraordinary puzzle!"

Now again he peered into the eyepiece of his telescope, squinting and screwing up his face in his intense interest.

"Oh, lovely," he whispered. "A lovely color. Bluish green — yet, not always — now pale — now a bit deeper. Variations could be the effect of our atmosphere, however. But what *could* the green be? Not chlorine, thank goodness, because then my boy, whoever he is, would be unable to breathe. No — some infinitesimal plant matter, perhaps? Another mystery. But it's beautiful, and to those living on Basidium, a blessing. For that green mist must curtain the eyes of the Basidium-ites against the too-brilliant nearness of the earth. Marvelous, indeed, are the arrangements of nature!"

Mr. Bass smiled to himself, plucked his pencil from behind his ear, and made the following notation in his Basidium notebook:

"The deliverance of my people on Basidium is near," he wrote, "because today there appeared in the newspaper my want ad for a small space ship. Who has seen it? What boy (only one boy, of course — the *right* boy) will have seen, or been shown, that notice? He will be lying in his bed at this moment wondering what it could possibly mean. But being the right boy he will have his plans all drawn and they will be ready, even now, on some shelf or table in his darkened room. Soon I shall meet him. Who is he, I wonder. What is his name? Oh, I am like a child myself, for I can hardly wait to find out!"

Then little Mr. Bass, still smiling, closed the notebook, laid down his pencil, turned out the light, and went off to bed.

CHAPTER 3

Spare Parts

V ERY, VERY EARLY the next morning David was to be found hunched over a number of old can and bottle boxes near the incinerator at the bottom of the Topman garden. Dr. Topman had cleaned out the garage on Sunday, and when that happened no sensible person would believe the number of perfectly good things that got thrown away.

Now began such a rattling and scraping and banging that John, the rooster, and Mrs. Pennyfeather, his wife, craned their necks and stared, and their children all ran up to the fence of the chicken yard and stretched out their beaks in amazement. Up from those old can and bottle boxes there flew all sorts of odds and ends.

"Nope, don't think so," David would mutter to himself, for he had a surprisingly clear picture in his head of exactly what he needed. Then, excitedly, like a dog digging for a bone, "Yep, yep, just the thing for the instrument panel!" Now there would be absolute silence while he sat back on his heels and pondered over an old cog wheel, or a coiled-up spring covered with graphite. Then, presently, "Oh bo-o-oy, a barometer! Now why d'you s'pose Pop threw *that* away? It's broken, but I betcha it could be fixed. And here's a toggle switch — at least I *think* it's a toggle switch. Then I've got to have a pressure gauge. Very important. Can't get along without a pressure gauge."

This went on for quite a while, and just about the time David had all the spare parts he needed, who should come along but Chuck Masterson. Chuck could be a lot of fun and very helpful sometimes. But other times Chuck was stubborn. Just let David get an idea about how something should be done, and Chuck would think it should be done just the opposite way. And he wouldn't give in. He'd say David was stubborn and wouldn't give in either, so there were days when they never got anywhere.

All the same, they were the best of friends. They were both in the same grade at school.

18

David was tall and quick, with freckles and sun-bleached brown hair that flopped over his eyebrows. Chuck was shorter and squarer with brown skin and dark hair. David liked to plan things and draw and talk, but Chuck just liked to get right in and *do* them without saying much. Right now, Chuck's father and mother were away on a trip, so Chuck and Cap'n Tom were living alone.

"Watcha doin'?" said Chuck.

David turned up his streaked and sweaty face and squinted at Chuck sideways. He seemed to consider something with great seriousness, and then finally to make up his mind.

"Chuck," he began solemnly, "have you and Cap'n Tom talked much lately about space ships and traveling to the moon and life on other planets and all that?"

"Sure," said Chuck, "lots of times." Now David stood up, leaned close to Chuck, and stopped a moment before he spoke very, very slowly, with stern and narrowed gaze.

"Did he read out to you a piece in the paper last night about a small space ship being wanted by a certain Mr. Tyco M. Bass — a little notice printed in green?"

Chuck's eyes grew big. "A space ship! Gee whillikers — no!"

"He didn't say a word?"

"Nope. But if he'd seen it, he would have."

You see, Cap'n Tom believed in all sorts of things — flying saucers and such as that — and sometimes he'd stand out on the beach at night and stare and stare up into the sky for minutes at a time to see if he could spot anything. But he never had. All the same, Cap'n Tom loved to yarn about discoveries in space and flying to the moon and what life on space stations would be like just as much as he loved to yarn about all the weird things that had happened to him at sea.

"Well, listen, Chuck," said David, "it's a kind of mystery, because my father says *there is no such street as Thallo Street,* the place you have to bring your space ship to when it's finished."

"Then," said Chuck in his downright, sensible way, "why don't we go try to find it?" But David frowned at that and didn't answer. He just began picking out all the biggest tin cans he could find and tearing the paper off of them.

"Not going to," he said finally. "There's a Thallo Street somewhere, all right, or that notice wouldn't have been in the paper. Besides, it'd

20

take too much time to go off and hunt for it, and I've got to hurry."

The truth of the matter was, David didn't want to admit his real reason for not settling the mystery. You see, *if* there were no Thallo Street, and therefore no Mr. Bass, and therefore no reason to build the space ship, he couldn't have stood it, because he was as stuck to the idea of that space ship as a nail is stuck to a magnet. Now he looked up at Chuck again and fixed him with a grave stare.

"Chuck," he said, "would you like to go off on an adventure and have a chance to do a good deed?"

"What kind of an adventure?" asked Chuck cautiously.

"I don't know exactly — but I'll bet it'll have something to do with space."

"I think we ought to go and find that street first," said Chuck stubbornly, "or else what's the good of beginning?"

"O.K.," said David, picking up his box of spare parts, "I'll just build the ship myself, and if it's the best one I'll go off on the adventure alone."

Oh, but Chuck couldn't bear that! If there was

one thing he hated more than another, it was being left out of whatever was going on.

"All right, *all right*, then — how do we begin?" And he looked angry, but you could tell he was going to stick until he found out what this was all about.

"Bring that box of tin cans, will you, Chuck?" grinned David, pleased as Punch he'd won Chuck over. "I thought we could do our building down in that cave on Cap'n Tom's beach." Now he started away down the path leading to the sand, which stretched away in a curve at the bottom of the cliff beneath the Topmans' back garden. Beyond the row of wind-twisted old Monterey cypresses that bordered the path stood Chuck's house.

"Will the adventure be *dangerous?*" shouted Chuck all at once, hurrying along behind with his box of tin cans rattling and banging. "Will we have to go out beyond where planes go?"

"Sh-sh-sh!" hissed David furiously, turning on him. "It's a *secret!* And don't you tell *anyone*, because other kids might come and spy, and copy our design. And don't tell Cap'n Tom, because he'd be full of ideas and want to help, and this is just for boys eight to eleven with no grownups nosing in. Now I've got all the spare parts here, and those tin cans have to be flattened out so's we can nail 'em onto the outside of the ship. All we need is wood."

Chuck stopped in the middle of the path and stared into David's box, which was full of what looked like junk. How on earth could anyone build a space ship out of that, he wondered. He shook his head, and yet — and yet already he could feel himself beginning to warm with excitement. He could feel himself beginning to think about that adventure and to hope that he and David would be the ones chosen to go.

But all the same, flattening out dozens of tin cans to cover the outside of the space ship appalled him!

"Hey, David!" he yelled suddenly, lifting his voice sharply above the rumble of the waves that came creaming and spreading in all up and down the shore. "*Listen,* Dave! Cap'n Tom has some sheets of tin, or some kind of shiny stuff, over in his boathouse. Leftover pieces, all shapes, not very big, but a lot better'n tin cans. We could finish off with tin cans. And Dave, he's got all sorts of laths and two-by-fours, and he's even got some curved-up ribs left from a little old sailboat he took apart — you know, ribs steamed up just the shape of a space ship. Dave, *they'd be perfect!*"

David caught his breath. He could scarcely believe their good luck. Curved the shape of a space ship! How many other boys in Pacific Grove or in Monterey would have grandfathers with ribs of old boats lying in their boathouses, and big beautiful sheets of shining metal just waiting to be used? Maybe dozens of boys! And all of them, at this very moment, might be asking their grandfathers for the loan of those old boat ribs and those enormous metal sheets.

"Oh, c'mon, Chuck, hurry, *hurry!*" he cried, his voice high with impatience and urgency. "We haven't got a moment to lose. We've got to find Cap'n Tom. Chuck, *we've got to be first!*"

CHAPTER 4

Dr. Topman
Pays a Visit

THE BUILDING of that space ship, down in the cave, took exactly three days. Now, this may seem a very short time to the average person, but it was almost beyond belief how some strange power took hold of the hands of the two boys so that their fingers, all of themselves, seemed positively to fly from one thing to the next. Not once did Chuck and David have to stop and ask themselves how the building of the space ship should go.

Every now and then bigger boys, from over on the next block, would go by down at the far end of the beach. Then Chuck and David would watch to see if they intended to come near, and were ready, if they did, to trick them away. But those bigger fellows seemed to have business of their own.

Nobody came near. Cap'n Tom seemed, for

those three days at least, to be totally uninterested in taking the boys fishing. Nor did he inquire as to what, exactly, was being done with his wood, with his boat ribs, and those odds and ends of sheet metal which he had said they could have.

It was a funny thing about Cap'n Tom. When they'd gone to ask him for the wood and the pieces of metal sheeting, he had been splicing rope. He did this very carefully and deliberately, and with such neatness that you could hardly tell where one piece of rope left off and the other began. He was a nice plump man with snapping blue eyes, pink cheeks which were red-veined from all the storms he'd been in, and thick, crisp, curling white hair. Sometimes when you asked him a question he didn't answer right away, and so it seemed as if he hadn't heard you. But he never missed a thing.

Now when the boys had made their request, they waited with beating hearts, for they'd expected all kinds of awkward questions. But Cap'n Tom squinted at his rope in silence. Then at last — just as if he were giving them permission to use his nails or a hammer — he'd said slowly, not looking at them:

"We-ell now, seems to me I can't think of a thing I need those old boat ribs for, or those

26

pieces of aluminum sheeting. No sir — not a thing!" Then he'd slid each of them a kind of quick, sharp, sparkling look out of the corners of his eyes, and smiled to himself. And the boys had stared at each other across the comfortable roundness of his stomach, thanked him breathlessly, then stolen quickly away — quickly, quickly, before he could change his mind or ask why they wanted the ribs and the sheeting. But he never had asked, and their private affairs and what they were up to seemed not to be on his mind at all.

Only Mrs. Topman was worried. "David!" she would call after him in exasperation at noontime, "you haven't eaten *half* your —" but he would be gone. There was nothing she could do. "The boy's possessed!" she would cry to Dr. Topman when he came home in the evening.

"He'll get over it," Dr. Topman replied, but he looked grave. He had a thin, kind face with sparse hair on top. And whenever he looked grave, he looked very, very grave indeed. His patients always said that they would have trusted him to take off their heads, if he'd needed to, look inside, and pop them back on again. "By George, I do hope the whole thing isn't a joke," he said.

27

"It isn't," replied Mrs. Topman, and she didn't know how she knew this, but she did.

"I keep meaning to hunt up Thallo Street," said Dr. Topman on that last morning, "then somehow I forget. But there's no person by the name of Bass in the telephone book and no Thallo Street on any map. I tell you, my dear, there *is* no such place. I think that on my way home tonight I shall have a good look for it."

So he did.

And the same evening at dinner Dr. Topman was strangely quiet. He'd chew for a while, then he'd stare at the tablecloth with the oddest expression on his face.

"Is anything wrong, dear?" inquired Mrs. Topman anxiously.

"No," said Dr. Topman hastily. "Nothing — nothing at all."

"What are you thinking about, Father?" asked David.

"Thinking?" said Dr. Topman in surprise, just as though he'd never done such a thing in his life. "I'm not thinking. I'm just eating. And you would do well, young man, to follow my example. Stop asking questions."

"O.K.," said David. "But I have something to

28

tell you, Father. We finished the space ship!" For some reason, Dr. Topman's face grew red.

"Did you now, David!" he exclaimed heartily. "Well, that's fine." He coughed. "That reminds me," he said. "I happened to go by this — this Thallo Street on my way home to look up your friend, what's-his-name."

David stopped chewing and looked at his father with his mouth half open. Then he swallowed.

"You mean," he said in a low voice, "that you've *seen* Mr. Bass? You mean he's real, then?"

"Real?" repeated Dr. Topman briskly and matter-of-factly. "Of course he's real. Why wouldn't he be? Anyone would think there's something peculiar about all this. Why would there be? There was a notice in the paper, wasn't there? Someone had to *put* the notice in the paper, didn't he? Well, he did. Nothing strange about that. And this Thallo Street is a little, short street only about six blocks over from here. Can't think why I've never seen it. You go up to the end of it and there's Number 5, perfectly plain and ordinary. I couldn't find anyone about, so I walked through the garden and around the house — and then came right out again."

David's eyes were like saucers. "You *did*,

Father?" he breathed. "And what — I mean, who — what happened?"

"Why, nothing happened. What should happen? It's a nice little house with a garden — that's all."

"That's *all!*" wailed David. "But what was it *like*, Father? Didn't you even *see* Mr. Bass?"

"Er — after a manner of speaking, yes. I thought I'd just take a peek in the window, as I couldn't rouse anyone, and would you believe it, the window was flung right up in my face, and a head appeared. I was absolutely startled out of my wits. I must admit I've never been in such an embarrassing position in my life!"

"Oh, but Father," persisted David in anxious desperation, "*was* it Mr. Bass? What did you say to him?"

"Very little. I was in rather a hurry. Now kindly get on with your dinner."

CHAPTER 5

Mr. Bass—
at Last!

It was a glorious morning when Chuck and David set out for Mr. Bass's, guiding their space ship between them on its four-wheeled carrier, David in front and Chuck behind. The sun danced on the waters of Monterey Bay so brightly it hurt one's eyes to look. The sea gulls on the shore were already getting their breakfasts, and everything was bright green and blue and white: green gardens, blue bay, and white gulls and fishing boats.

As for the space ship, it was truly awe-inspiring. It was long and smooth and cigar-shaped, just as David had planned it, with the big window in front made of fine thick plastiglass which David's mother had given them. On the right side was the door, which could be bolted tight shut when you got inside. At the rear was the sturdy, four-bladed tail, level on the end so that the space ship could be upended to stand firmly. For the ship was separate from the carrier and could quite easily be slipped off when the time came to blast away. Over its entire surface it was covered with cleverly fitted sections of metal sheeting, so that it glistened and gleamed in the morning sun like some marvelous, silvery fish. How beautiful it is! David said to himself as he stared at it. He hadn't realized before just *how* beautiful — and how big!

Now you know, that was a funny thing. David turned around, as they went along, and gave the space ship another good look just to be sure about its size, and there was Chuck having a stare at it at the same time.

"Chuck," said David, "does it seem bigger to you — that is, sort of bigger than it was last night?"

"How could it be?" said Chuck scornfully, but he didn't sound at all sure of himself.

"Well, it couldn't be, really," returned David

hastily, "but all the same, it seems to me it does."

Chuck didn't answer. He just kept walking along with his eyebrows drawn up in a puzzled frown, and every now and then he'd give that space ship a sidelong, wondering glance. He couldn't understand it. He thought they'd planned to have the ship eight feet long, but surely it was longer than that now!

How everyone gawked at them —boys on bikes and workmen hurrying along, and women going up the street with bags of groceries in their arms. They'd look. Then they seemed to come to and look *again*, blinking and craning their necks as long as the big space ship stayed in sight. What fun it was to knock the grownups off their pins like that!

Meanwhile, they were coming nearer and nearer to that short street, six blocks from David's house which his father had said would be Thallo Street. And they were so excited by this time that they forgot to wonder any more about the size of the space ship.

"Is it pretty soon now, Dave?" asked Chuck, and he sounded just a little bit scared.

"Next block, Chuck. Funny, isn't it, no other fellows are bringing their space ships? *Somebody* must have seen that notice besides me."

"I still think it could be a big, awful kind of joke on us," said Chuck in his solid, fateful way. "I *told* you we should have hunted up the street first and talked to this Bass person."

"You never did either say anything about talking to him," said David angrily, and he knew he was angry because he was worried.

So now they came to the end of the sixth block — and there, sure enough, was Thallo Street, a little, short, dead-end street, but plain as plain could be. They turned along it. All was perfectly quiet. Not another boy did they see. Not a person did they meet.

"There — Number 5," whispered Chuck. And they both stopped. It was the last house, tucked away in a mass of trees. Through the thick greenery they could just make it out, very small, almost circular, it seemed to be, with a roof somewhat the shape of a mushroom and with a strange sort of ridge running over the top. Tacked to the white picket fence was a sign printed in queer, straggling letters. They bent down to read, and it said:

Then, so unexpectedly that they jumped, there came a soft, high, delicate voice.

"Why, come in, boys, come in!" And the voice seemed so distant, as if a wind from a far place had carried it to them, that they could scarcely believe their eyes when a little old man poked his head out of the bushes right where they stood — a little old man not an inch taller than they were.

"Come in, do," he urged, waving them eagerly forward. But at the same time his glance lit upon the ship. "*Oh!*" he cried. An amazed smile broke over his small, wizened face, and now he hopped right out of the bushes and whipped open the front gate.

"Oh my, oh *my!*" he exclaimed, his voice trembling with pleasure. "What a surprise! What a beautiful piece of work — beautiful — just *beauti-ful!*" He rubbed his palms gleefully together, and then was suddenly right beside them, devouring the space ship with his great, round, pale brown eyes. "Oh, I never in the world expected anything like this. It's far beyond my wildest dreams."

35

He smoothed a long, thin, weblike hand over the ship's glossy surface, leaned down and peered within, fetched a long breath, went round to the other side, peered some more, and then drew a deep, satisfied sigh. "Goodness," he went on, as if to himself, "just imagine — the boys of today — mere nippers, too — simply to think of it. All so quick — practically in the wink of an eye. Marvelous! But now, we must introduce ourselves. I am, as you have perhaps guessed, Tyco Bass."

He gave a quaint, formal little bow and held out his hand to each of them.

"How do you do, Mr. Bass," returned Chuck and David in chorus, and then:

"I'm Chuck Masterson," said Chuck, his heart beating fast.

"And I'm David Topman," said David, and thought how like a whisp of cool air was Mr. Bass's hand.

"Which of you was it who saw my notice?"

"My father showed it to me," said David, "and I cut it out and kept it, and drew my plans that night."

"So I thought it would be," murmured Mr. Bass, and he looked on David with the greatest affection, "so I thought it would be. You know,

David, it must have been your father who came by last night just to be certain his son was not being fooled. I should so much have liked to talk to him about you. But I'm afraid I shoved my window up too suddenly, for he vanished before I could so much as call out to him. A great pity! But now we must go in and begin our planning at once, for there isn't a moment to lose — *not a moment!*"

CHAPTER 6

The Discovery
of a Satellite

WITH THAT, he turned and hurried through the gate, and the boys hurried along behind. Not for a second could they take their eyes from him, for never in their lives had they seen such a strange little man. It seemed as if he might float away at any moment — or was it, David wondered, the way the breeze played through his few thin locks and lifted out the funny long gray gardening coat he had on! Then what a huge, round, pale head he had, and what a very small face, and enormous, liquid eyes, and what thin, spindling arms and hands!

"Now then," he said, darting round to a side door of his house, "just slip your beautiful space ship in here so she'll be snug and safe. This is the cellar, where I grow my mushrooms. My family, for as long as I can remember, has earned its living by growing mushrooms for the markets, and so I do too. Fortunately there is a very obliging man down the street who takes me in his car to market three times a week with my boxes."

So the space ship was rolled into the darkness. There the boys caught just a glimpse of innumerable tiny white shapes that spread away and away — a glimmering of hundreds of little bald heads that seemed miniatures of Mr. Bass's own. Then the door was closed and locked just as if the cellar contained a treasure, and the boys were led round to the front of the house again and ushered into the living room.

Outside the windows the trees pressed close, and inside a wavering, sea-green light filled the room like water. Maps of the heavens covered the walls, together with five or six large pictures in color of the planets of our solar system. They were paintings. But they were so real that you would have thought someone with a camera had stood on the very surface of those distant worlds and taken color photographs.

There were the rings of Saturn, as though you had stood on Saturn itself and looked up into the sky. There were Martian landscapes, and a terrible picture of Mercury all baked and cracked with heat. There were two awesome pictures, one of Mars, an enormous pinkish orb webbed over with its green canals, hanging in the black sky above Deimos, its satellite. The other was of a huge, yellow Saturn, belted with darkness (the shadow of its rings), seen from the surface of its rocky little satellite Mimas.

The boys stared at the pictures in silence. Then David turned to Mr. Bass, who was watching them with the greatest enjoyment.

"Did you paint all these, Mr. Bass?"

"Oh yes," said Mr. Bass lightly, as though it were nothing — nothing at all. "It's a little hobby of mine, to paint what I can imagine of the planets according to my observations and my mathematical calculations. But now," said Mr. Bass, settling himself in an enormous chair that made him look smaller than ever, and waving the two boys to a low couch, "now — at last — I will tell you what has been on my mind."

The boys sat down, scarcely able to believe that the great moment had finally arrived. Indeed, they could scarcely believe in Mr. Bass, and David kept wanting to reach out a finger and touch the little man, but of course he did not.

"First," said Mr. Bass solemnly, "I want you to

know why I put that notice in the paper. You see it has always seemed to me that I am so different from other earth dwellers, that I must be of another kind of life entirely. Not just of another race, you understand, but of another *kind*. Doesn't it seem to you, Chuck and David, that I am somehow very different from other human beings?"

"Oh yes, Mr. Bass!" agreed Chuck and David so heartily that their faces turned quite red with embarrassment. However, their vigor didn't seem to bother Mr. Bass in the least. He chuckled and nodded.

"Absolutely different," he agreed. "What is more, all my people have been different. And they have always kept themselves to themselves, with their own customs and stories handed down from father to son.

"Well, so you see, this set me to wondering if we, my people and I, might perhaps be *of another planet altogether!*" Chuck and David gasped. "Yes, it seemed to me that that might be very possible — but of *what* planet? I asked myself. Surely it would have to be a satellite of earth's, and what is more, a satellite not too far off on which a race of people had developed, a race somewhat like

41

earth people, of course, and yet — different. Different, you see, as I am different." He paused and gazed at the boys and then held out his incredibly long, thin fingers, which looked positively greenish in the soft, swimming light.

"But Mr. Bass," exclaimed Chuck, "how could some of *your* kind of life get *here?*"

"Why, in the shape of a spore, I should imagine," replied Mr. Bass lightly. "So our strain of life must have begun, carried here in some mysterious fashion across those intervening thousands of miles from that other planet. The chance is one in billions, and yet there have been such exceedingly rare occurrences. You notice I said 'in the shape of a spore.' I might have said seed, but in our case, being Basidiumites, or Mushroom People, I have to say spore. Because, you see, my people develop as mushrooms do.

"Well," went on Mr. Bass, "supposing then that there *is* such a satellite — why, I asked myself, has it never been discovered? There seemed to be no answer to this question — unless" — and here Mr. Bass's eyes narrowed shrewdly and he leaned close and held up one spidery finger — "unless," he breathed, speaking very slowly, "this little satellite is *invisible* to astronomers who per-

42

sist in searching the skies with their *ordinary* telescopes —"

The boys stared at him, scarcely breathing.

"The kind that, no matter how big and powerful they are," broke in David, bursting with excitement, "*still* can't find your satellite!"

"Pre-*cise*ly," beamed Mr. Bass. "Therefore, there was only one thing for me to do — I had to invent a filter to go over the eyepiece of my telescope which would enable me to see light rays in a way that they have never been seen before.

"I knew that first of all I would have to make a complete study of light, which I did. Then it came to me one night that perhaps the polarization of light in combination with some sort of stroboscopic mechanism might possibly do the trick. Well," said little Mr. Bass, "in the first place, I had to discover whether I must use plane polarization, elliptical polarization, or circular polarization — or perhaps some unheard-of arrangement of all three. And secondly, this particular filter had to be combined in a certain way with my stroboscopic mechanism, which, I assure you, is such a mechanism as has never before been seen on earth."

43

"What's a strobo —— stroboscopic mechanism, Mr. Bass?" asked Chuck intently.

"A stroboscope, Chuck, is an instrument that interrupts light periodically. But that, in my case, is putting it far too simply. For I had to create new substances to take care of the special purpose I had in mind, some which I think I can truthfully say have never been guessed at in the study of light."

"But what *are* they, Mr. Bass — and did you have to use all three polari —— polarizations, or only one — and *which* one?"

"Ha," said little Mr. Bass, his eyes twinkling. "Hm-mm. Well, that is all very difficult, very complicated, you know." Very secret, I think he means, David said to himself. "At any rate, days passed, and nights," went on Mr. Bass, "for I was so impatient at feeling myself on the brink of discovering my ancient homeland that I scarcely stopped for food or sleep. One small problem, which I had thought would be the least troublesome, proved to be really staggering. But at last I hit on the answer that I had known almost instinctively would be there — because it *had* to be there! Into my metal holder I slipped the polarized filter and attached the stroboscopic mechanism, on which I had had to make many, many fine adjustments. Now this metal holder was fitted over the eyepiece of the telescope, and the switch controlling the mechanism was plugged in. Slowly — slowly I searched the heavens, and then I knew that the moment for which I had waited and worked so long had finally arrived."

At the memory little Mr. Bass seemed quite overcome. For a second or two he could not speak.

"My dear friends," he said, his eyes shining, "I cannot tell you all I saw that night. Venus, for instance, appeared in an entirely different aspect, for, you understand, my filter enabled me to see it as no other astronomer has ever done. But I was not after Venus — no, no. Patiently I moved on — until — one morning, very early, I came upon my little satellite!

"Yes, there it was, only 50,000 miles out from our earth, roughly a fifth as far away as the moon, in a position in space that all astronomers would swear is empty.

"And upon beholding it, so tiny, so beautiful (I shall not attempt to describe it to you now), I named it Basidium-X. Basidium, because I am certain it is peopled with Mushroom folk like myself, and X because it is still unknown — unknown, that is," and now Mr. Bass smiled a radiant smile, "except to ourselves, Tyco Bass, David Topman, and Chuck Masterson!"

David and Chuck stared at Mr. Bass in stunned silence. Then at last David managed to speak.

"Mr. Bass, do you suppose we could — that is, will there ever be any chance of *our* taking a look at Basidium?"

"Ho," cried Mr. Bass, "I should say there will be! Indeed, it is high time for me to show you my own small, private observatory."

His own small, private observatory! One wonder, marveled David to himself, was being piled upon another.

CHAPTER 7

The Marvelous Filter

Mʀ. ʙᴀss went over to a door and held it wide.

"Go carefully," he warned. "These stairs are rather steep and tricky."

There before the boys wound a flight of narrow steps, and up they went with Mr. Bass after them as light and quick as though he were a boy himself. At the top, they came into a cozy little room all outfitted with everything that anyone who has longed to study the stars could want.

"Here is my star camera," said Mr. Bass. "On its plates I take photographs of the stars and planets. And this is a spectroscope. Do you know what a spectroscope is? Well, it is an instrument that tells you, by the colors in its rainbow color bands, what other heavenly bodies are made of. Oddly enough (or perhaps not so oddly), they are made of exactly the elements which the earth is made of. Then, this is a thermocouple —"

47

"Thermocouple," repeated David and Chuck, testing the word on their tongues and thinking what a funny one it was.

"Yes, and it tells me the temperatures of the heavenly bodies. I am very happy to report that the temperature of the atmosphere on Basidium is cool and delightful — just right for a visitor — or visitors — from earth." At these words, Mr. Bass glanced at Chuck and David with twinkling eyes, and a little shiver — half awe, half quivering suspense — rippled up and down the arms of the two boys. "There, of course, is my telescope." It was tilted up and pointing to the dome of the little room.

Now, without a word, Mr. Bass touched a hidden button. Slowly, slowly, a strip of the domed ceiling crept back. And at that moment David remembered the peculiar ridge he had seen outside that ran over the round roof of Mr. Bass's house.

"Next," said Mr. Bass, "the filter." He went to a little wall safe and from it took out a small round object to which a long cord was attached. One end of the cord he plugged into an electric socket and then clamped his filter snugly over the eyepiece of the telescope. Now he perched himself on his high stool and slowly and carefully began manipulating a number of knobs and dials.

"Why do you have to plug your filter into a wall socket, Mr. Bass?" asked Chuck.

"Because the stroboscopic part of my filter works electrically," answered Mr. Bass in an absorbed voice.

The two boys watched him tensely. How eerie the little room was, filled from floor to ceiling with row upon row of books, and rather dim and dusky except for the mote-filled strip of sunlight that drifted through the narrow opening.

"Let's see now, should be about 280 degrees azimuth, elevation three degrees," muttered Mr. Bass. Slowly, searchingly, the whole body of Mr. Bass's telescope moved back and forth, its eye pointed heavenward. At last Mr. Bass turned and held out a hand. "Here," he said, "take a look at this."

David stepped up and took a look. At first he could see nothing at all, but then, gradually, what looked like a tiny greenish dot became visible. Now Mr. Bass turned one of his dials again, and lo and behold, the greenish dot swam closer until it became about a third the size of a full moon, shining very, very pale and ghostly, a watery, silvery, bluish-green orb.

49

"Basidium-X!" announced Mr. Bass, his voice full of emotion. "Basidium, the invisible planet, seen for the first time in the history of the world by the earth dweller, Tyco Bass."

"And seen now," breathed David, his voice scarcely above a whisper, "by a second earth dweller, David Topman."

"Let me look!" cried Chuck at last, rudely shoving in. But he had to be forgiven, for David had looked a long, long time, with his mouth open, after Mr. Bass conjured up Basidium.

"But Mr. Bass, how does the filter *do* this?" queried Chuck, one eye wrinkled up and the other staring and staring.

"Ah, that is the whole secret," chuckled Mr. Bass gleefully. "As you have perhaps guessed, I call it my Stroboscopic Polaroid Filter, and yet that name does not even begin to pin it down precisely. At any rate, it not only makes certain heavenly bodies visible, even in the daytime, which have never been visible before, but also enables our vision to penetrate whatever heavy atmosphere or vapors may surround them.

"One thing that has puzzled me is why the atmosphere of Basidium should be green. However, the right answer I can only learn after some visitor to the little planet has brought me back a sample of its air — in a canning bottle, perhaps."

"In a *canning* bottle!" cried both boys at once, snatched from the far reaches of space to a picture of their mothers leaning over steaming kettles and putting fruit into glasses.

"Why yes," said Mr. Bass with an elvish look, "that would seem to me a fine receptacle to bring back Basidium air in, with the top well screwed down. At any rate, Basidium *must* have air, and now I will tell you why I think this is so."

Mr. Bass perched himself on his stool again, and the boys sat cross-legged at his feet.

"You must know that we Mushroom People," began Mr. Bass, "are primitive in many ways. We catch one another's feelings instantly, and for the past week or two I have felt in my bones that all is not well. I cannot sleep at night for thinking about my people, and, curiously enough, my concern and my thoughts center on Basidium. This means, to me, that my people are there. It means that they are in trouble and that they are trying to get in touch with me. That is why I put my notice in the paper, for I knew that children could help me."

"But Mr. Bass," protested Chuck, "if you

51

wanted someone to go to Basidium, why didn't you get one of the big airplane companies to build a rocket ship for you, with lots of men and supplies, and scientists, and all like that?"

Mr. Bass closed his eyes for a second in horror, and shook his head and waved his hands about in the air.

"Dear me! Oh, no, no, no!" he exclaimed. "A huge rocket ship, even could it have been built in time, and all the great lumbering men in space suits with oxygen tanks and cameras and radar instruments, would have frightened the poor Mushroom People out of their wits. Then too," smiled Mr. Bass rather dryly, "what president of an airplane company would have believed me? You boys wasted no time in doubting. And, Chuck and David, you must *never* doubt anything I tell you. Remember that," said little Mr. Bass, leaning forward earnestly, "you must *never doubt.*"

Now David could feel himself edging up to the peak of this whole conversation, and his hands suddenly went damp and cold.

"The thing we'd like to know next, Mr. Bass, is — what do you want us to do?"

Mr. Bass's face at once became grave, almost stern.

"I should like," he said quietly, "for you two boys to dress very warmly, store your space ship with food, and set off this very night for Basidium."

For several seconds not a sound was heard in Mr. Bass's observatory but the rustle of leaves outside, a ripple of bird song, and the barking of a little high-voiced dog up the street.

"Tonight?" repeated Chuck faintly.

"But Mr. Bass —" began David, his hands getting colder than ever.

"Ah," said Mr. Bass sadly, "I'm sorry. I see that I am asking too much."

"Oh, no!"

"No, no, Mr. Bass, we *want* to go! We've *got* to go!"

"You have the courage, then?"

"Yes, sir."

"And you will tell your parents everything? I would not have you," said Mr. Bass, "take another step without their permission, not even to save my people."

"Well then," exclaimed Chuck in bitter disgust, "it's all off. My mother wouldn't even let me go to summer camp till I was eight, so what would she say about my going off into *space?* Cap'n Tom has to do just as he thinks *she* would, because she and my dad are away."

"They'll *never* let us," cried David, banging his fist down on his knee in a fury. "Even if we tell them the Mushroom People are in danger and need help, they'll *never* let us."

But strangely enough, Mr. Bass seemed not in the least worried about what Cap'n Tom and David's father and mother would say.

"I think," he told them comfortingly, "that everything will be all right. You'll see. And now there are several details we must get straight before you leave. First, and most important, is the matter of power for your space ship. Come along with me, now, and I'll show you one or two little arrangements I've been working on. Then we can finish fixing up your ship."

CHAPTER 8

Mr. Bass Does
Some Tinkering

Down in the cellar, Mr. Bass padded off into a corner. Presently the place was flooded with a soft, very clear light which revealed the most astonishing array of contraptions the boys had ever seen.

"Great jumping kadiddle fish!" shouted Chuck. "You must invent all *sorts* of miraculous things, Mr. Bass!"

"Ooh, yes, I suppose I do," replied Mr. Bass modestly. "But you see, most of my inventions aren't any good for production on a large scale, because I'm like one of those cooks who put in a little of this and a little of that and get the most delicious concoctions you ever tasted. But they can't tell anyone else afterward just *exactly* how they did it. Now there," said Mr. Bass, "is your rocket motor. Here," and he turned to his long, littered workbench, where lay two shining cylin-

55

ders, "are the fuel containers for your journey. The fuel in them is another invention of mine — but I assure you that this fuel, *incredibly* powerful, is like a special shade of paint. I don't imagine, for the life of me, that I could get just this mixture again."

"Will it work?" queried Chuck a bit uncertainly.

"Ho, of course it'll work!" laughed Mr. Bass, hustling over to the space ship with some long lengths of pipe and some wires and the shining cylinders. Then he went over to the rocket motor and, with the help of the boys, got it down off its shelf. "Now, I'll just put in this motor and hook up the fuel tanks. Then we'll be ready to put the sealer on your ship and store in the oxygen supply. Can't have you blacking out on the journey, can we?"

"No *sir!*" murmured David, as he watched with amazement how quickly and firmly little Mr. Bass set to work. To look at that small, frail man, you would never have imagined him capable even of tightening a bolt, or of being able to lift anything heavier than a glass of water. But in the wink of an eye he had the rocket motor in, and the cylinders installed in the rear of the space ship and connected to the motor by a lot of intricate-looking wiring.

"Gee!" cried Chuck in astonished admiration. "I guess you're a kind of genius, aren't you, Mr. Bass? Like Leonardo da Vinci. Our teacher told us all about him. He could paint pictures and think up inventions and make airships and everything, just like you!"

"Oh my," protested Mr. Bass, "I think that's going a long way, Chuck, to put me in the same class with such a great man. But I do hit on some rather interesting ideas now and then. Well, let's see now." Mr. Bass scratched his head and then went over to a large wooden vat. "Here are some brushes. We can all do this. Just slosh this stuff over the outside of the ship — over every single inch of it, now — and it'll be sealed up tight as a drum. It dries hard, like glass. Here we go!"

So all three of them, each with his big brush, painted the space ship with the fluid resinoid silicon (*with other ingredients,* David read on the label) from one end to the other, and right over the window, as Mr. Bass directed. And you could still see through it just as though the marvelous fluid were not there! Then Mr. Bass seemed to feel that the job was not yet finished, for he got inside the space ship and thoroughly painted the inner surface as well.

"That'll do it!" he cried, vastly pleased at the way the mixture had dried. "And what is most important, boys, is that now you will be absolutely protected from the lethal rays of the sun, which, unhindered by any atmosphere, could have penetrated the ship's walls and done you unimaginable harm. Amazing! If only I had put down what I did to get this substance, but all I have left of *that* experiment are a few scrabbly notes. Ah, well, it's no matter. Let's get on to something else."

Now he pointed out to them an object somewhat like a big coffee urn with a spigot at the side.

"This is your oxygen supply," he said. "Help me, boys, will you? This goes inside the ship, and I have arranged, by means of a mechanism on the spigot, that you will be supplied with just the minimum of oxygen necessary to keep you comfortable between the atmosphere of earth and that of Basidium. Now — here we go — heave up!"

All three together, the boys and Mr. Bass, heaved and shoved and got the strange-looking urn inside the ship and stored away in the rear.

58

"Turn the little handle of the spigot just before you take off," instructed Mr. Bass, "but don't forget to turn it back when you land on Basidium. You must not waste an ounce of your oxygen. And now," the little man went on, hopping down from the space ship and turning to face the boys as they came after him, "another matter" — and he held up that long first finger of his.

"It is *absolutely necessary* that you leave *immediately* on the dot of twelve, midnight." Mr. Bass fixed them with his huge, solemn, pale brown eyes, and for some reason the boys felt shivers go up and down their backs.

"Yes, Mr. Bass — immediately," said David.

"Yes, sir," said Chuck, and then couldn't help adding, "but why?"

"I will tell you," answered Mr. Bass, and he went over to his bench and picked up some papers all covered, the boys could see, with long rows of figures — rows and rows of them! Mr. Bass must have been busy for days working out awfully hard arithmetic problems, short division and long division and subtraction and multiplication and everything you could think of.

"You see," he said, "as Basidium is 50,000 miles out in space, and as you will have to travel at an average speed of 25,000 miles an hour, that means it will take you two hours to get there. Am I right?" The boys gasped and trembled, and then nodded without answering. "Now, I have calculated *precisely* the position of Basidium in relation to earth at two in the morning — two hours after midnight, that is. Therefore, if you do *not* leave at midnight exactly," went on Mr. Bass with a terrible look, "it is dangerously possible that you will not hit Basidium at all. *And* if you do not *leave* Basidium at exactly four tomorrow morning, according to our time, you will not contact the earth at this spot. Instead, you may land on the barren wastes of the Tibetan Plateau, from which no human beings could ever rescue you. Or it might be, you would miss the earth entirely and shoot on, far into the uncharted regions of outer space, where you would be lost forever. Have I made myself clear?"

The uncharted regions of outer space! David shuddered and thought how the barren wastes of the Tibetan Plateau sounded almost cozy and comfortable by comparison.

"All clear, Mr. Bass," he replied weakly, but Chuck only blinked and was silent.

"Good!" said Mr. Bass in a brisk, businesslike tone, as though he had no more than settled that they might land at Fishermen's Wharf instead of the corner drugstore. "I shall give you this paper, David, to be kept by you at all times. It has the position of the controls of the space ship — at what figures to set them on leaving earth, and then on leaving Basidium. Several thousand miles out from Basidium, the ship has to turn around in space in order to land tail down on Basidium — all ready to take off again, you see. Also, the rocket motor must be shut off so that the ship can go into free fall, that is, be drawn by gravity only, toward Basidium. The same turn in space, and the shutting off the motor, must take place when you are approaching earth on your return journey. But this you need not worry about. I have installed a surprisingly simple mechanism in the rocket motor which takes care of these matters."

David folded the paper carefully and put it in his wallet. Then he put his wallet in his pocket and buttoned over the flap.

"Now the next thing is," went on Mr. Bass, "who has a watch?"

Wordlessly, Chuck held out his wrist, around

which was strapped the fine, sturdy watch with luminous hands and figures that Cap'n Tom had given him for Christmas.

"Oh, capital!" exclaimed Mr. Bass. "Simply capital! And luminous hands into the bargain. Couldn't be better. I trust you will use that watch, boys, to the very best advantage. Because time, for you, will be a matter of life and death. This is all you have to remember: make your contacts *on* the hour. No matter what else happens, *be on time!*"

David was silent for a moment, and then the question that had been hovering vaguely but troublesomely in the back of his head got itself into words.

"Mr. Bass," he began, "there's something I just can't understand. How ever are we to talk to the Mushroom People? And if we can't talk to them, how are we to find out what's the matter and what we can do to help them?"

Mr. Bass smiled at David. "An excellent question, my boy. But I ask you to believe me: Everything will be all right. You and the Mushroom People will understand one another perfectly."

Now he held out a hand to each of the boys,

and they knew that their visit with Mr. Bass had come to an end.

"Mr. Bass," burst out Chuck, "why can't you come with us? You just *can't* stay behind. You're so wise, and know everything we ought to do — you've *got* to come!"

But Mr. Bass regretfully shook his head. "Oh no, Chuck, that is impossible," he said. "If I went with you, all would be in vain, for I am an adult. Don't you remember, I said that only children could do this thing? A grownup would spoil it — and besides, I feel that there is something else in store for me. Yes," and he looked away for a second with rather an odd expression, "I have a feeling that I must prepare for a very important event in my life here on earth. And that means there is a great deal to be done — dear me, yes, a *great* deal!

"Now, one last thing," finished Mr. Bass, "you must on no account forget the canning jar of Basidium air. Simply leave it uncovered while you do your work on Basidium, then at the end of the two hours screw the lid tightly back on and bring it to me. I am very anxious to analyze that air so that I can find out the mystery of its greenness.

And now, good-by, boys. The very best of fortune go with you!"

As the boys drew their space ship out of the cellar into the daylight, the sunlight flashed and glistened once more on its beautiful, silvery sides. How could it be possible, David asked himself, that that very night it would carry Chuck and him 50,000 miles into the cold and trackless dark? But — *You must not doubt,* Mr. Bass had said. *You must never doubt!*

At the gate, Mr. Bass stood beaming and waving as they went off down the street with their space ship between them. But then all at once he gave a loud, anxious cluck and darted out of his gate after them.

"Boys! Boys! Goodness gracious," he cried, coming up all out of breath, "I almost forgot. Disastrous! You are to remember to take a mascot. This is *most* important. A mascot. Will you remember?"

Amazed, the boys promised. But as they looked back after little Mr. Bass scuttling along with his gray gardening coat flapping about his knees and the few hairs on his bald head lifting in the breeze, they wondered just *why* it should be so terribly important that they take a mascot.

PART TWO

On Basidium

CHAPTER 9

Blast-off!

David opened his eyes, and everything in the house was dead still. He listened. Not a sound, except now and then the scratching of a bush against the side of the house. He leaned over to look at the clock by the side of his bed and it said a quarter past eleven. That meant he had just three quarters of an hour.

Quietly he slipped out of bed and, in a puddle of moonlight (for it was a fine, clear night), got into the winter clothes his mother had laid out for him. This was a thing he still couldn't understand — how calm she had been, putting out his corduroy trousers and his plaid woollen shirt and his muffler, and all the time talking matter-of-factly about the journey and wishing him *bon voyage!* Now he zipped up his leather jacket and quietly — oh, ever so quietly — stole into the kitchen and got the biggest bag he could find from the middle drawer on the right side of the sink.

Then he got a loaf of bread and put it in, and also two boxes of cookies. Next he opened the refrigerator door and got out some tomatoes (but put them back because they might get squashy), a head of celery, some carrots, a head of lettuce, five wienerwursts, a package of sliced ham, a package of sliced cheese, and some oranges. Then he opened the drawer under the refrigerator and got out four bananas and six apples.

He looked in the bag, but his heart sank, for it didn't seem nearly enough for a voyage into space. So he opened the cooler and found a package of dates, a box of raisins, a cellophane bag of shelled nuts, another box of cookies, a bar of cooking chocolate, some candy, and a jar of peanut butter.

That would have to do, David said to himself, even if they did starve before they got to Basidium. But he was terribly worried, so he got out the last loaf of bread from the bread bin. Then he started to pick up the bag — but how surprising! It would hardly budge.

With a tremendous effort, he hoisted it up into his arms, staggered out the back door, and just made it out to John and Mrs. Pennyfeather's coop before he had to put it down again. Maybe it was all the winter clothes he had on that made the carrying of that bag so hard, because certainly there was scarcely enough food in it to last them out the first five hundred miles.

Then on he struggled, and there, at the bottom of the cypress path, was Chuck. He too was breathing heavily.

"Couldn't find very much," hissed Chuck out of the shadows. "But I guess it'll have to do." David hoisted up Chuck's bag and it was, if anything, weightier than his own. All the same he felt gloomy. He wondered what it would be like to starve to death in the middle of space.

Down at the cave, however, where they could just make out the soft glimmer of their space ship snug inside, David got that tight feeling in the depths of his stomach that meant he was unbearably anxious for the adventure to begin. They put their bags down and went in.

So, one on each side of the space ship, they wheeled it down onto the sand. They wedged their heavy bags of food under the seats, and then, with much struggling and hauling and heaving, got the space ship upended near a huge rock.

The beach was flooded with moonlight (for the

moon was within two nights of being full), and in that clear, soft brilliance the rock looked like an enormous, shaggy giant with some object from another world resting in its grasp. Shadows were deep black. And half shadowed, half revealed in its gleaming beauty, with its slim nose pointing straight upward, the space ship seemed already eager to be free of the earth. It seemed almost alive and to be tensely awaiting the moment of take-off. The boys stared for just a breath while the waves fell upon the sand, and somewhere far off a single shore bird gave its long, plaintive cry. Then Chuck turned.

"I remembered my flashlight, Dave," he said in a low voice, "but I forgot the auto robe — I should have brought that too in case it gets awfully cold." Forget! Remember! An appalled look came over David's face.

"The canning jar!" he groaned. "I forgot it, Chuck. The canning jar for Basidium air. What'll Mr. Bass say? It's too late to go back for it now." But Chuck gave his arm a comforting shake.

"Never mind, Dave. I brought some sugar in a canning jar," he said, "and we can just dump the sugar out."

David felt as though he had been stretched

like an elastic band and then snapped back again. "O.K., Chuck," he sighed. "Let's go. Are you ready?"

Chuck gave a look, slow and solemn, all around the beach and then up at his house as though he had an idea he might never see them again.

"Yes," he said at last. "Yes, I guess I am."

But just then, just as they were about to climb up the rock and get into the ship, David had another awful thought.

"Chuck! The mascot! We forgot to bring the mascot!"

"Oh, golly," exclaimed Chuck in despair. "*Now* what're we going to do? We haven't got *time*. It's —" and he pushed back his sleeve and peered at his watch — "it's just ten minutes of midnight."

"Mrs. Pennyfeather!" cried David. "How about Mrs. Pennyfeather? It wouldn't take a minute to get her."

"Or John maybe," said Chuck, scrambling up the beach after him.

"No, *not* John," puffed David, running as fast as the sand under his feet and his thick shirt and leather jacket would let him. "He's no good. You need somebody friendly."

Up at the chicken coop, David unlatched the gate and stole carefully inside. He knew that if he woke John and Mrs. Pennyfeather and their children all at once, there would be the most awful cackling and squawking and goings-on. Silently he drew back the door of the hen house and put his head in.

"Mrs. Pennyfeather!" he whispered. "It's just me — David."

"Quawk!" cried John indignantly, and you could tell by his tone he'd been startled out of his wits.

"Qua-a-ahk?" asked Mrs. Pennyfeather sleepily. And from the other perches there came disturbed rustlings and queepings and drowsy murmurings.

David crept toward Mrs. Pennyfeather's perch. He put his hand out and gently stroked her back and head and then as gently lifted her into his arms.

"Qua-a-ahk," remarked Mrs. Pennyfeather in her soft, comfortable voice, and she didn't seem in the least disturbed or annoyed, so David stole out of the hen house again to where Chuck waited.

"Get a bag of feed, Chuck," he said. "There're

three in there — medium-sized, not too heavy. You can drag it."

"Oh, *gosh*," protested Chuck, "you mean all the way to the *beach?*" But all the same he went on in and presently returned dragging a dark, sagging shape. "Why a whole bag?" he whispered furiously.

"Don't know," said David. "Got a hunch we'll need it." Off they went.

It was a frightful job getting that sack of feed up onto the craggy rock. Once on a level with the space ship door they just had to let it slide down inside and pray it wouldn't damage the oxygen urn. Chuck climbed in with Mrs. Pennyfeather, and then David got in and they strapped themselves down tight and safe.

"You'll just have to keep holding Mrs. Pennyfeather, Chuck, because when we get out far enough she'll float around, and that might upset her. Now for the controls." He got Mr. Bass's paper out of his wallet, and by the glow of Chuck's flashlight he read out the directions and set the controls accordingly. "There, now — that puts us on the beam, on the what-do-you-call-it, the right *vector*, and we don't have to worry."

But then, just as David was folding up the paper again and putting it in his wallet, Chuck struck his hand to his head in horror.

"*Oxygen!*" he cried out. At once he put Mrs. Pennyfeather into David's arms, unstrapped himself, dropped down to the rear of the ship, and in a moment or two there started up a small whistling, like a peanut wagon. Phee-eep, phee-eep! went the escape valve in the urn. And this small whistling kept up for the whole of their journey. Once more Chuck strapped himself down.

"Time, Chuck?"

"Midnight — *pre*-cisely!" And they grinned at one another because that was Mr. Bass's word.

"Ready, Chuck?"

"Ready," returned Chuck in a low voice.

"Well then," said David, and his blood seemed to halt in its flight, "let's go!"

Now the boys crouched down as though they expected to be struck. David pulled back the stick and pressed the button, and with a roar and a great, crackling burst of flame the space ship shot straight up — up — up over the moonlit ocean.

For a few seconds it was terrifying! Everything seemed to happen at once. First there was the blasting roar, and the boys were flung backward in their seats so violently by the forward impact of the ship that the breath was knocked out of them. And at the same time poor Mrs. Pennyfeather lost her wits entirely and squawked and flapped and flew in their faces, beating her wings so wildly that they were completely blinded by her.

But then, as the space ship shot smoothly upward and there was nothing to be heard but the steady peeping of the oxygen urn, they got their breaths again and Chuck collected the terrified and trembling Mrs. Pennyfeather. Gradually their hearts stopped pounding and they became calm.

Now, surely, everything had been taken care of. Now at last they could look out of the window in peace and see how they were ascending, straight and swift and sure, into the blue-black, silent midnight skies. And there still hung the moon, David noticed in wonder, looking at them as serenely as though an absolutely unheard-of event had not just taken place.

CHAPTER 10

Into Uncharted Regions

For a long time the boys said nothing, but sat without moving, without speaking, staring all around. Firmly and noiselessly their ship sped on — and yet, David asked himself suddenly with a sharp pang of fright, why should their flight be noiseless? He listened. And there was nothing — nothing but the little whistling of the urn. Was something wrong then?

He had just started to cry out in terror when his mind replied to his fear. He recalled something he'd read. They had broken through the barrier of sound, and at this appalling speed — a speed at which most human beings on earth would have no least desire to travel — he and Chuck were leaving sound lagging far behind. He was stricken with awe and relief, and, feeling too exhausted to tell Chuck all this, turned to the window once more.

Now as they left the earth's atmosphere, the two boys stared in wonder at the stars, those far-off suns, billions and billions of miles away. Red and white and blue-white they burned. Like points of fire they blazed in the velvety firmament, and the greatest of them were Vega, Deneb, Antares, Arcturus, Spica, and Regulus. At this hour of midnight, the Milky Way was just rising along the eastern horizon, and, of its constellations, the Northern Cross, with its brilliant star Deneb, was to be seen in the northeast, and Scorpius, jeweled with red Antares, was in the southeast.

High in the mountains, David had seen the stars sparkle as he had never seen them in the city. But now he knew that neither he nor any other earth-bound creature had ever seen them in their true glory. And because he would have liked his mother and father to behold this sight too, he thought of them. He thought of his mother sitting on the side of his bed and saying quite calmly:

"But of course you must go, David. If Mr. Bass says his people are in danger, there is no reason you shouldn't try to help them, though it may be very difficult. What did you say the name of the satellite is?"

"Basidium-X," David had reminded her. "Or at

least that's what Mr. Bass calls it. Basidium because he's so sure the Mushroom People live there, and X because it's still unknown — that is, to everybody but Mr. Bass and Chuck and me," he finished proudly. "We don't know what astronomers or space men will call it when they discover it ten or twenty years from now."

"Ten or twenty years from now — I see," his mother had said in a faint voice. Then she was silent as though she were trying hard to arrange all this in her mind. "Well, David," she said finally, "you just go to sleep now, and perhaps you'll find your little planet."

Then she'd gotten up and, just as though she were getting him ready for a trip to the mountains, gone about laying out his winter clothes, humming to herself. He hadn't been able to understand this. She hadn't seemed worried at all.

"Was Cap'n Tom worried, Chuck?" David asked suddenly. "Did he make any fuss about your coming along?"

"No, he didn't," replied Chuck, and he sounded puzzled. "He didn't bother a bit. He just looked at me sort of sideways as if he wondered whether I was telling a whopper or not. Then he chuckled and said, 'Go to it, Chuck. Go to it —

78

and good luck to you! Keep a sharp eye to starboard, son, and don't go to sleep at the wheel.' And I said, 'Do you *mean* it, Grandpop? D'you mean I *really* can go?' And he said, 'Of course you can go! Now you get to sleep. Sleep's good for a man who's got a long voyage ahead of him.' Then he went off whistling, just like I was going fishing or something. Funny, isn't it?"

Yes, it was a funny thing. But here they were, and everything was all right at home. No one was worrying, no one was sitting up stewing about them, and that was a good feeling.

"You know, Chuck, I've been wondering about this word Basidium — what it's got to do with Mushroom People. So before I went to bed, I had a look in my dictionary. And you know what, Chuck? It's in there. It means — now, what was it? — I memorized it." And here David screwed up his eyes in order to remember better. "It means a form of spore-bearing organ char-ac-ter-istic of all ba-sidio-my-cetous funguses — I mean fungi."

"Wow!" said Chuck. "*What* a mouthful! And fungi —"

"— are rusts and smuts and mushrooms and puffballs. I looked that up too. But first it said,

79

any of a group of *thallo*-phytic plants, including the rusts and smuts and puffballs and mushrooms!"

"Thallo Street!" exclaimed Chuck.

"Which probably means," went on David, "that Mr. Bass's family here on earth have lived there for years and years — maybe gave that street its name because of the kind of work they've always done. Still, it's awfully funny we've never noticed it before, isn't it?"

"Seems to me," said Chuck, "there're lots of things that are funny about Mr. Bass — not funny to laugh, but funny peculiar." Then he yawned and yawned until his eyes watered. "Wonder what Mr. Bass is doing now — right this minute. I'll bet not sleeping. I think he sits up all night and reads and never needs any sleep at all."

"Well, I'll bet he's sitting on that high stool of his in his observatory, charting our course on his map of the solar system. And I'll bet he knows exactly — I mean precisely — where we are." Then, thinking of where they were, thousands of miles out in space already, a question came into David's head. "Chuck, why do you s'pose Mr. Bass said we'd *have* to travel at 25,000 miles an hour?"

Chuck grinned. Now he'd have a chance to show off a little. David didn't know everything.

"Cap'n Tom and I talked about that last night. And *he* said that we couldn't get away from the pull of the earth's gravity unless we traveled seven miles a second. *And* — when you multiply that all out, you get 25,000 miles an hour. See? If we didn't travel that fast, we couldn't get away from the earth. We'd just fall back in toward it."

Now, thinking of Mr. Bass's wonderful inventions — like the fuel that was blasting them toward Basidium — and of his uncanny knowledge of so many things, David all at once remembered something else that contradicted this and made his heart sink. On the radio, faintly from the other room just as he was falling asleep last night, he'd heard storm warnings.

"All fishermen and owners of small craft in Monterey Harbor are urged to put out extra anchor and chain," said the newscaster. "This is going to be a humdinger, so the weather man tells us, and it'll be here early tomorrow morning!"

But Mr. Bass had said nothing about a storm. Was it possible he hadn't known? Perhaps there were many things, after all, that Mr. Bass didn't know. And yet — there was something he had told them very gravely and seriously: never to doubt.

David frowned and drew a deep sigh, turning to Chuck. But there was Chuck, his head slipped down against the window, fast asleep. And in his arms, fluffed into a warm, round shape of softness with only the tip of her red comb showing, was Mrs. Pennyfeather fast asleep too.

CHAPTER 11

The Pale Planet

Davɪᴅ could not think what had happened to him or where he was. He sat up and rubbed his eyes, and the first thing that struck him was the color of the light. It was green — a real green — wavering, misty. It was like clouded sea water illumined by sun. But if it was light, then it must mean they were near something that was reflecting light.

David caught his breath and leaned to look out. There, a great way below them but dimly visible through the winding mists, hung a small planet, so small that he could see how the edge of it curved, far, far rounder than he had seen the dimly lighted edge of the earth curve against space.

Already, while they had slept, their space ship had turned so that its tail pointed toward Basidium. Now it was in free fall — falling into a landing on the little planet instead of blasting toward it nose-first as it had been doing when they were awake. The rocket motor, at the time of turning, had automatically switched off. So now David, according to the directions Mr. Bass had given him, switched it on again to slow down the ship's hurtling fall.

"Chuck!" he cried eagerly. "Wake up, Chuck, wake up! We're almost there!" Ah, but how strange his words sounded to him, and how strange his voice — high and delicate and far away like the tinkle of wind chimes. Could this be he, David Topman? "Ah-ho!" he cried out, testing himself anxiously. "Hey! Hi!" But it was no use. Whatever he said, no matter what sound he made, he still sounded a great way off. Chuck stirred, then raised his head and blinked.

"Where — wha — what is it?" he asked in confusion. Then he sat up. "Why, it's all green. The light —"

Yes, and Chuck's voice too sounded peculiar, the voice of another being entirely than the Chuck David knew. And then his words — what could be the matter with them? Chuck started forward and pressed his face to the window and looked straight down. "Dave!" he cried.

"It's Basidium — we're there, Dave! We're there!" Then he turned, a startled look on his face.

"Yes," said David, and now he knew how it felt to have his heart leap in his throat. "It's the little planet just our size." But Chuck was staring at him.

"Dave," he whispered. Then he tried it out loud. *"David Topman!"* He put his hand to his mouth. "We sound different," he got out at last.

"I know," David answered quietly. "Perhaps it's the atmosphere." But all the same, he had a feeling it wasn't the atmosphere at all. And then, as the small world below them swung up nearer, he had an awful moment of uncertainty. "There it is, Chuck. But what if the people aren't people? What if they're — ?" He couldn't even begin to imagine what impossible sort of being they might be. Of course, as Mr. Bass was a Basidiumite, though of a race that had lived long on earth, surely they would resemble him in some way or other. "But what if they're awfully — *primitive,* just the *beginnings* of a Mr. Bass? What if they only make noises?" he finished with a shudder. But Chuck's eyebrows drew together

85

as they always did when he was trying not to be bothered about something.

"Quit worrying, Dave. What's the use of worrying about that now? We're here, aren't we?" he said, in his solid, sensible way. "And we understand each other, so maybe we'll understand them. Maybe they'll sound — windy, like we do. It sure is a funny thing," he finished slowly and wonderingly, and he shook his head back and forth in amazement.

Neither of them spoke any more, but stared down in silent fascination as they came nearer and nearer to the pale green surface of Basidium. Now the ship came to rest with a slight thud and David turned off the motor. With huge eyes the boys peered out at what lay about them.

Through the wavering green light they made out that this entire world was pale. Over its surface grew what seemed to be spongy moss, and from it sprang primitive-looking growths that were like fern trees, with feathery fronds and trunks as smooth as bamboo. Yet these trunks were not the color of tree trunks at all, but as pale green as the rest of the plants. And there were mushrooms — hundreds and hundreds of mushrooms wherever you looked! Grayish white and pink and cream they were, every kind you could imagine, some huge and towering, with great, thick, fleshy stems, and some slender, and some small and delicate, myriads of them growing out of the moss. When the boys opened the door of the space ship they were met by a dampish smell — the smell that comes to you from an old rain-soaked log when you pull off one of those ruffled, fanlike fungi, or when you break a mushroom apart.

"I'll turn off the oxygen urn," cried Chuck in his new high voice, dumping the dazed and sleepy Mrs. Pennyfeather into David's arms and then wrenching away at his strap. Quickly he dropped down, turned off the urn, and was back again. "We'll have to jump out," he exclaimed eagerly, poised at the open door. "But it looks soft. Here, give me one of those bags." David let Mrs. Pennyfeather flap down to roost on the oxygen urn, then laid a hand on Chuck's arm.

"And how are we going to get back up again, Mr. Smarty? What do we do, fly?"

"No," said Chuck, vastly impatient. "I'll boost you up — the soles of your Keds'll help. Then you can reach out and pull me up — I've got Keds too. We'll *do* it! Quit fussing around, for the love of Mike. You're always *worrying* about something."

Out went Chuck like an eager bird, clasping his great bag of supplies, and then David, taking a last look at Mrs. Pennyfeather and clasping his bag, jumped too. It was only about six or seven feet down, and when he landed he smelled the cold fungusy smell of the bruised and crushed growth beneath him — almost like moss but spongier and wetter.

"Come on, Chuck — leave the bag here. We've got to hurry. Remember, we've got *just two hours,* and then we've got to be back on the dot of four in the morning. Say, what time is it now?" Chuck peered at his watch and then grinned.

"By golly," he said appreciatively. "It's three minutes after two. And we've been staring around for just about three minutes. Mr. Bass is a wizard!"

Then, quite calmly, as though he had all the time in the world, Chuck plopped down crosslegged on the moss and proceeded to root around in his bag for something that would please him. Out came pickles and hard-boiled eggs and a package that looked as if it must hold five or six sandwiches. When it was undone, it turned out that that was exactly what the package did hold, and they were thick and stuffed to bursting with different kinds of fillings.

"Got up about an hour ahead of time and made these," announced Chuck with immense satisfaction. "Going to have a big feed now." David couldn't believe his ears.

"But we've got to find the Mushroom People!" he exclaimed, about to explode with exasperation. "We've got to get *on* with things!" Chuck continued his chewing. He seemed absolutely unmoved by David's desperate expression.

"Got to eat first," he said, his cheeks bulging. "Starved. Do what you like." So David furiously resigned himself and picked up one of Chuck's sandwiches and started in. Suddenly, in the middle of a big bite, Chuck burst out laughing so hard that David, with a chunk of sandwich in one hand and a stick of celery in the other, simply stared at him.

"What's so darned funny?" he wanted to know.

"Us!" shouted Chuck, only his shout didn't sound natural, but like a soft, far-off shout. "It's us," he shouted, "you and me sitting here having a picnic on a planet 50,000 miles out in space, eating sandwiches and celery and hard-boiled

89

eggs just like it wasn't a bit different from a hike at Big Sur." David looked off.

"Yes, it is kind of funny, isn't it?" he said. But somehow he didn't feel very much like laughing. It was all too — too unbelievable. He wanted to pinch himself to think of the two of them here in this pale, green, spongy place and not knowing at all whether the living things they would meet could speak and think and feel as they did. He took another bite, but he felt queer inside. "I guess just now, Chuck, I'm not very hungry."

Then he lifted his head and listened. *What was that?* And then Chuck must have heard, for he too lifted his head and listened. Over beyond the horizon, so astonishingly close after what they had been used to on earth, came the sound of — could it be? — yes, wailing and moaning and groaning! And then there came words, and some of them sounded like "Aye, oh — aye, aye, aye, aye!" or maybe "Yai, yai!"

"People!" whispered Chuck hoarsely.

"Shhh! Listen!"

"Yai, yai — oh, yai, yai, yai!"

Nearer came the cries, the wailing and sobbing and groaning. Then David pointed, silently. And as Chuck turned, two old men, apparently as like little Mr. Bass as they could possibly be, came slowly from over the far side of the sky line. They were clutching their heads and beating their breasts, and spreading their arms wide and turning their faces up to the sky and then staggering on, dissolved in grief.

CHAPTER 12

The Wise Men
Who Weren't Very Wise

Bᴜᴛ they were people — people like themselves, with bodies and arms and legs and heads and faces like their own, or at least as near like their own as to make no difference. David and Chuck drew together, standing silently. The two little men, upon suddenly spying them, stopped, stared, and then as though hypnotized came slowly — sl-ow-ly — forward.

As they came nearer it was seen that they were not as like Mr. Bass as they'd first appeared, but rather like an exaggerated Mr. Bass. Their heads were larger and more domelike, and their faces were smaller and paler, almost gray. Their eyes were huge, great round brown staring eyes — gentle, frightened eyes like a tarsier's, thought David, and he had to hold his breath in wonder and surprise.

92

How were they dressed? Well, it looked to David as if the cloaks and skirts of these two little beings (not quite as tall as he and Chuck), draped about them in a kind of Greek way, were made of soft plastic. They seemed to be made of the material raincoats are made of nowadays, that smooth rubbery stuff you can almost see through. It fell in nice folds, and one little man's skirt and cloak were soft cream, and the other's were pale, pale pink — exactly the shades of the great mushroomy plants that were growing all about.

Now the two little men came right up to them, their eyes peering and peering, first at the boys and then at the great space ship towering behind them. Their long pale hands were held up in front of them as though fending the boys off, and perhaps the space ship too, as though they wanted not to be hurt.

"But we wouldn't hurt you!" burst out David, because he had to answer that frightened look.

Now the two little men seemed to relax somewhat, and they took small, quick looks at the boys' clothing, then drew their eyes back to the boys' faces as though they felt they'd been impolite.

"I am Mebe," said one of the little men, almost in a whisper, and took another awed, careful look at the space ship as though he thought it might be alive — as though it might jump round and eat him.

"I am Oru," got out the other little man, and he too took a sideways, awed look at the Thing.

"But it's dead," laughed Chuck. "It isn't alive, like we are, I mean. It just goes when you want it to." But still the little men would not come nearer, nor look at the space ship straight on. "If you're afraid of it, how did you have the courage to come over to us at all?"

It seemed to David that Mebe and Oru had been drawn over the ground as though pulled by something they couldn't help, even though they were scared to come.

"We *had* to see," said Mebe. "We just *had* to. We always do have to see everything."

"That's what I thought," grinned David.

"Why were you crying?" asked Chuck then, just as he would have asked a small boy who's been hurt.

"Because we're to have our heads cut off in the morning — *squirp!*" said Oru, making a swipe across his throat with his finger. Then the two little men wrung their hands and began groaning all over again.

"Squirp!" repeated David in horror. "You mean you're to be *beheaded?*" Mebe nodded.

"There's no help for it," he said tragically, his huge eyes swimming with tears. "The time is too short to get to the bottom of our Trouble now, and we can't think fast when we're worried."

"But why are you to be beheaded?" cried Chuck.

"Because —" began Oru.

"The Great Ta," said Mebe, "ordered that if —"

"Now you let *me* tell," interrupted Oru angrily. "You always want to tell everything and you get it all mixed up."

"So do you," snapped back Mebe. "I never knew anyone to get everything so mixed. The only time you are sensible is when you inscribe in your Rolls of Wisdom." But David put up his hand.

"Now please listen," he said firmly. "We've been sent here by one of your kinsmen on earth to help you in your Trouble. The only way we can help is to be taken to this Great Ta. And while you take us there, you can be telling us the whole thing. Now, Mebe, you begin, and when you're through, Oru can tell us about the Great Ta and what kind of person he is."

"But before that," put in Chuck, wanting to get first things first, "just who are you two?"

"We," said Mebe and Oru together, "are Ta's Wise Men."

"Only," said Mebe sadly, "we haven't been very wise. We have failed. But now, I'll tell you about the Trouble." And all four of them began walking off together. "You see, to begin with, there's a plant — a magic plant — that grows high in the mountains —"

"The jar!" shouted David all at once, clapping his hand over his mouth. "The canning jar — I forgot it again, Chuck. I just don't think I'll ever get it safely to Mr. Bass with the Basidium air in it." He dashed back, grubbed around in Chuck's bag, got out the canning jar full of sugar, dumped the sugar in a white heap on the moss while Mebe and Oru stared, then set the jar open, with the lid nearby, in one of the corners made by two tail blades of the space ship. "There!" he said. "Now, Chuck, *don't let me forget to take it home.* O.K. — here we go, we've got to hurry." Once more they started away and Mebe continued:

"As I said, there is this magic plant that grows

96

high in the mountains. It is a food we have to have or we die, because it has something in it — we don't know what. And it grows in only one place. It looks somewhat like the other foods we eat — there — and there — and there —" He pointed about, but the plants he pointed to all looked the same to David, the same mushroom-like growths. "But this plant is *not* the same as the others. When we don't eat it, we grow grayish, as you see us now. A healthy person is pale green.

"But the terrible trouble is — we have no more of the magic plants. What few are left, we are giving to the children that they may live. They are the only ones of us now who are a fine, healthy green, as you will presently see."

"But Mebe," cried Chuck, "*why* are there no more of these plants you have to have? What happened to them? Will there never be any more?"

"You see, they all died —"

"There came a great hotness —" broke in Oru excitedly, waving his hands upwards, and Mebe turned on him in a fury.

"*I'm* telling, *I'm* telling!" Then he turned back with offended dignity. "As I said, this plant grows high in the mountains at the Place of the Hidden

Water. And the interesting thing is that the smell there has always been very thick and strange —"

"— *sickening!*" remarked Oru.

"Silence!" barked Mebe. "We will probably have to take you there if you are to help us at all. Then you can smell the smell for yourselves and see where the plants grow, and maybe tell us what you think about the water that comes up out of the ground. Always, enough of these plants have come up in a season to give us a good amount to dry until the next Time of New Growth comes around.

"But the Great Ta, in his enormous wisdom, had often asked himself — *and* us — 'What if some sudden change in the air destroyed our precious plants before we could gather enough of them to dry and store away?' So he ordered us to think about this and to find what wonderful treasure they hold that our bodies need. Then if our supply failed, or the air changed, we would know how to grow more or grow them in other places." But now Mebe and Oru stared shame-facedly·at the ground.

"And *did* you think?" asked Chuck.

"Ye-es, we thought. But not enough. We kept putting off and *putting* off because the puzzle was so hard. And the Great Ta would call us to him and we would have no answer — until finally —"

"— finally —" groaned Oru —

"— finally the thing came that Ta had feared. The air changed. It grew hot, so hot that we could not work. Our people sat around gasping, and the wet ran down our faces. When the gatherers of the precious plants went to the Place of Hidden Water, all our crop was dead, black and slimy. Not one was left — not one. A few dried plants from the last Time of New Growth are all we have left."

"And so you see," finished Oru, "we are done for." And with glassy eyes, he again drew a long, spindly finger across his thin, spindly neck. David shuddered and thought what a wee little whack it would take to finish him off. "But now," went on Oru in a speech-making voice, and you could tell just how much he had been looking forward to his turn, "*I* will tell you about the Great Ta. He is the Wisest One of All — the only one of our people who is able to understand the deep and difficult things we two put into our Wisdom Rolls. He is —"

But just then, both little men looked on ahead

99

and stopped, and the boys looked, and there stood a personage only slightly taller than themselves, but whom they knew at once to be the Great Ta because of a certain unmistakable kingliness about him. He was dressed no differently from Mebe and Oru except for a necklace of great, richly colored stones around his neck and a long, gleaming staff in his hand.

He stood and looked at them levelly and calmly, with no change of expression even though, of course, he'd never seen anyone like them in his life. Mebe and Oru bowed low to the ground, so Chuck and David did the same thing.

"I am Ta," said the man in deep tones. "I greet you."

"I'm — that is — we're —" began David, his heart thumping in his chest, "I'm David Topman," he said, and how peculiar his own name sounded to him all at once!

"I'm Chuck Masterson," added Chuck, sounding rather stifled.

"Where have you come from?" asked Ta in his booming, regal voice. "You are strange ones."

"We come from earth, sir," said David. "We came in a space ship because one of your kinsmen on earth said that you needed help."

"Earth? What is this earth? And what is this space ship you speak of? I do not know these words. Come closer and tell me these things." So then David and Chuck approached, and Ta seated himself on a rock.

"There is the earth," David told him, and he pointed up to where, glimmering vaguely beyond the greenish mist, loomed a huge round shape many times larger than the sun, which was shining upon earth from the other side of the sky.

"Ah, yes," exclaimed Ta, looking up, as did Mebe and Oru, whose mouths were hanging open. "You come from there — from our Great Protector. If the Protector had been between us and the Hot One, we should not be in our present danger."

"Your Protector is the earth, our home. And the Hot One is the sun, but you couldn't live without the sun."

"You are wrong," boomed Ta. "The Hot One did us the evil. And, of course, those two foolish creatures there, my so-called Wise Men. But they shall learn that it does not pay to be foolish."

"You are cruel!" burst out David. "You're cruel to behead them! What good will it do you to

101

take their lives? You're all going to die anyway."

Chuck gasped in horror and Mebe and Oru seemed to shrivel. They hid their faces, terrified one should speak to the Great Ta like this. But Ta gave a slow smile.

"You have courage, Strange One from the Protector. But they must die because they have failed."

"Yi, yi!" cried Mebe and Oru softly, and they beat their breasts and bowed their heads. "Yi, yi, yi!"

"Anyway," said David, "we've been sent to help, so we've got to hurry and maybe we can save them as well as the rest of you. Great Ta, will you take us to the Place of the Hidden Water so that we can get on with our job?"

CHAPTER 13

The Place of
the Hidden Water

Tᴀ rose.

"We shall go," he said, "and as you speak of this place, it means that Mebe and Oru have at least had the good sense to tell you the story so that I shall not have to. Come! There is no time to lose."

Now, with his kingly stride and using his great staff to speed him along over the ground, his necklace of marvelous many-colored stones swinging from side to side on his chest, Ta started away. He gestured to the boys to walk by his side, but little Mebe and Oru scuttled along behind.

"Great Ta," began David with respect, "there is something I must ask you. You say all the time, when you're speaking of the plant mystery, that you must *think*. And Mebe and Oru said it too.

103

But haven't your Wise Men ever made *experiments* to solve puzzles?"

"Experiments! What is this word?"

"Why," said David, having in mind those laboratories to which his father had taken him in hospitals, "*you* know — where they have things in glass jars and make mixtures and heat them to see what happens. Or they let things stand around to see if they change, or feed them to rats and mice to see what the results are."

Ta looked utterly blank.

"I do not know what you mean," he replied. "You speak of strange happenings and use strange words. We think and think. My Wise Men put down what they think in the Rolls of Wisdom, then read aloud what they have written. And we talk about these writings."

Now David and Chuck stared at each other with the same blank expressions on their faces that had come over the face of Ta.

"But *then* — !" they both exploded at once.

"How do you *get* anywhere?" exclaimed Chuck.

"You'd just end up right where you started," cried David.

"*If* you don't work with the thing that's caus-

104

ing the mystery," said Chuck, "like these plants, for instance, what good does it do you and your Wise Men to just write what you already know, and then talk and talk about what you've written?"

"Sometimes it does good," returned Ta in his calm way. Then he looked off into the distance to where, through the winding greenish mists, the outlines of a small city were coming into view. And as he gazed away with half-closed eyes, he seemed to be going over in his mind what the boys had just said. "But perhaps," he went on, "you have a new thought which I and my Wise Men have not come to yet — the thought that we must work with the thing *itself* that is causing the trouble."

Now Ta was silent, and because the boys knew that in that great head of his something wonderful might be going on for the future good of his people, they too were still.

In a few minutes more they arrived at the little city, where a few of the Mushroom People came out to stare at them as they passed. At the sight of the two boys they shrank back amazed, and two or three ran away yelling and waving their hands about their heads. Children clung to their mothers' robes, and, just as Mebe had said, they were a nice, healthy green, whereas all the adult Mushroom People were gray.

"Never fear," boomed Ta, "never fear. These two have come from our Protector to save us. Come close and greet them!"

So, gradually, some of the more courageous ones came close. They could not take their enormous eyes from Chuck and David, but mostly they seemed to want to touch the boys' clothing, so Chuck very kindly took off his plaid woollen jacket and held it out to them. Timidly, as though they thought the jacket might explode, or fly away, or turn suddenly into something else, they put out their webby hands and rubbed the jacket sleeve between their long, thin thumbs and first fingers.

"I, too, have wanted to put my hands on your robes," admitted Ta, smiling, "but I thought that you might be offended." So now he, as well as his people and his Wise Men, felt of Chuck's jacket and then of the material of the boys' shirts and shoes and trousers.

"It is so strange!" they all cried, shaking their heads. "So strange! We don't understand how they could have happened."

106

For a moment David thought of trying to explain, but when he pictured sheep, and how you got wool, and fields of cotton, and cotton mills, and looms with threads spinning back and forth, and manufacturing plants with hundreds of people sewing and cutting and putting on buttons and zippers, he heaved a huge sigh. Imagine explaining a zipper to Mebe and Oru! Why he couldn't have explained a zipper to himself — he was sure he couldn't. Probably even his father or Cap'n Tom couldn't have explained a zipper!

"But we must go!" cried Ta suddenly. "Away with you all!" And the Mushroom People fled back to their funny little low, round, igloolike houses like crumbs before a wind. "We must be on our way!"

After they had left the small city, which was no more than a clump of these igloos — built of blocks of what looked like pale, porous rock — the ground became rough. It was no longer covered with the spongy moss that had made their walking so easy, but was now bare earth and rock, and the going was uphill. Steeper and steeper became the path, and around them, on all sides, rose the great thick-stemmed mushrooms, and other peculiar plants with pale, branching

107

arms covered with what looked almost like spongy leaves.

"May I ask — how do you make your robes, Great Ta?" asked David.

"We use the flesh of those bilba trees you see there," answered Ta, waving his hand toward the huge mushrooms. "We break them down and pound them and mix them with a liquid we make of the juices of many plants. When this mixture is almost dry, we roll out the substance flat and very, very thin, and after a time it is ready to be made into robes for our people."

How quickly Ta walked, and as they went along, David could hear Mebe and Oru scuttling behind like rabbits, puffing and blowing.

Now the path became steeper than ever, but up went Ta, sure-footed and quick, between the huge, overhanging rocks. Now that no one spoke, and they went leaping upward in silence, David began to notice what looked like tiny batlike birds darting high overhead. And once or twice he thought he saw birds (at least they *were* flying — or getting through the air in some fashion) that were like small lizards, for they whipped after them long, naked tails as they flashed from one plant to another. And then once, dimly

108

through the mists and the thick growths, he saw a dark animal shape crashing and lumbering away from them.

"Morunbend," remarked Ta, looking back for an instant.

"What did you say it was, sir?" asked Chuck excitedly, his eyes widening with eagerness in the hope of getting another view of the mysterious creature.

"Morabun!" David thought Ta called out, but he couldn't be sure, and so he never did learn the name of the beast.

Now David and Chuck were gasping. The green air swam before their eyes, and the sweat ran down their faces and down their arms, cold inside their clothing. But Ta remained as calm and unruffled as though he had been strolling across a flat plain. He stopped and looked at them.

"It is not much farther," he said, and he pointed ahead with his staff. "Smell the air. Can you get it — the peculiar odor?" Now little Mebe and Oru came puffing along, and they too sniffed.

"That's it! That's it!" they cried.

Oh, what *was* the smell? It was faint, but how familiar it was. It was not exactly a smell he liked,

David said to himself, and yet it was connected with something he *did* like. What could it be? He turned to Chuck, and there was a look on Chuck's face as though he too knew that smell, as though he had smelled it many times before.

On up they went, and now the path became dangerous and frightening. It was so narrow that the boys could hardly pass along it sideways with their backs to the steep, damp cliff and their faces turned outward. Below them plunged a terrible, dark ravine, the bottom so far down and so thickly filled with the green, moving mist that it seemed as if a ghostly river wound below them.

Ta called back cheerfully. They were almost there, he cried, and his voice echoed among the rocks. Presently, to Chuck's and David's enormous relief, they came out into a high upland meadow. On three sides rose steep cliffs. Away on the far side of the meadow Ta disappeared and Chuck and David hurried after. Now they started down into a steep gorge. At the bottom of the gorge the smell, which had been getting stronger and stronger and which David still could not name to himself, became overpowering. Here, indeed, in this damp, dim place, the smell

110

was so thick that David and Chuck had to put their hands over their noses.

"What — is —" gasped Chuck from behind his hand.

"Don't — know — terrible —" returned David from behind *his* hand.

"Here — here is where they grew," cried Ta, and he made a wide sweep of his arm around the gorge. The boys looked down at the floor of the place and saw that it was covered with a black-ish growth which was nothing but slime in many spots. When they knelt down, the blackish growth turned out to be hundreds of small shriveled plants — black in death, and useless.

But how damp the ground was, and when the boys wet their hands and smelled the dampness, there was that sharp, penetrating odor. The boys stood up, facing Ta.

"You call this the Place of the Hidden Water," said David. "That means that the water that feeds your plants comes up from an underground spring or river." Ta nodded, watching their faces keenly and steadily with his huge, piercing eyes. Simply with his gaze he seemed to be trying to drag the answer to this mystery out of them.

"We know this smell," announced Chuck. "We

111

know it so well. And we don't like it, but we can remember something at home that has this smell faintly, and whatever it is *there*, we *do* like it. But what is it? What *is* it? We can't think!"

Now you should have seen the faces of little Mebe and Oru! How they brightened — how they lit up. They came and stood in front of Chuck and David, clasping and unclasping their funny, long-fingered hands.

"Oh, you will help us," they cried. "We know you will help us — you'll think of the name of this smell!"

But Chuck couldn't stand the sight of their joy.

"Don't be so sure of us," he protested in desperation, "don't be so *glad!* What's there to be glad about, or hopeful, or *anything?* We only remember the smell. And what if we do remember what the smell *is,* how in Basidium is that going to help us?" Again, as it had so many times before, a look of puzzlement came over the wizened faces of the two little men.

"What is this Basidium you speak of?" questioned Mebe. But Chuck simply made a motion of despair and turned away.

"*Silence!*" roared Ta suddenly. "Enough wasting of time —"

"But Great Ta," broke in David all at once, "I *do* have a thought. If these plants grow only in this damp place and are watered by this underground spring, they must get what they need from the spring. Have you drunk the spring water to see if it might give *you* what you need?" Ta silently and majestically waved his hand toward his two Wise Men, and his lips curved in a rather ironical smile.

"Oh yes," said Mebe and Oru, "yes, *we* have, what little we could get. But it was awful. We were sick to death," and here they shook their heads and rolled up their eyes and put their hands over their stomachs as though they had suffered great pain and inconvenience from drinking the potent water.

"I *think* I understand," said David, frowning in a weighty and solemn way as he had seen his father frown when he was thinking something terribly important about a sick patient. "The water has in it other things *as well* as the one thing you need to keep you healthy. And it's the other things that make you sick." Chuck was frowning too, and then his face lighted.

"That's it, Dave!" he cried. "That's it! But the plants, as they grow, take only the one thing the

113

Mushroom People have to have." Then he sighed. "But that doesn't get us anywhere," he finished disgustedly. "We're right back where we started."

But Ta did not seem in the least disgusted or discouraged.

"You are very wise," he said in his calm, level way, "very wise indeed. I should like you to stay with me forever, for I have never heard thoughts follow one another so beautifully, in such neat steps, as they have come from your lips. You are far wiser than my Wise Men," and he turned and bent a terrible look upon those two unfortunates, who lowered their heads and twisted their hands together.

"But we can't stay, sir," exclaimed David anxiously. "We have to leave in a very short time — we've got to hurry! The only thing to do now is for you to take us back immediately and have Mebe and Oru read to us anything from their Rolls of Wisdom that might help or give some clue. We might come across something that will set us on the right track. But don't be hopeful," he ended gloomily. "Please don't be too hopeful."

Without a word Ta took the lead up the steep side of the gorge and out across the upland meadow. Now it seemed to take longer than before to wind their slow, perilous way along the narrow path above the ravine and down through the great rocks to the level land again. But perhaps it was because the boys were beginning to be uncomfortably aware of time.

"Chuck," cried David as they hastened along, "it's getting dark — darker and darker!"

Yes, it was, but what a strange darkness, for it was rather a kind of soft, green silveriness. Through the winding mists of the planet, which had now completely lost the glow of the sun, the huge shape of the earth was becoming clearer. It was like a moon seen through fog — but what a giant moon, what a stupendous, overpowering moon! On the other side of the sky was a smaller silveriness which told where the real moon was.

"Dave," said Chuck in an awed voice, "just think how it would be if Basidium weren't covered with this greenish mist. Why, the poor Basidiumites would hardly ever have any dark. If one side of the planet weren't in the sun, then there'd be the earth sending down its earthlight — not warm, of course, but awfully bright — and so big when it was right overhead, it'd be about ten times as big as the moon!"

"Yes," breathed David, staring up, "what a

115

queer business it all is." And they both stopped for a minute to gaze at the luminous shape of the earth hanging above them. Then they started forward again, still staring, so that they almost plunged from the cliffside.

"Watch!" cried Ta in alarm. "You must watch — you must look where you go!"

"But we can't *miss* the earth," Chuck said, hurrying on. "That's one thing sure. Even if we don't leave Basidium exactly on time, we'll still hit it somewhere — at least, I should *think* we would."

"Somewhere!" exclaimed David, aghast. "You mean the barren wastes of Tibet?" He shivered. "What time is it, Chuck?"

"Quarter after three," reported Chuck briefly. "Three quarters of an hour before we've absolutely got to go. We'll never make it, Dave — I mean, we don't stand a chance of helping Ta's people."

"No," answered David in a low voice so that Ta shouldn't hear, "no, it doesn't look like it, does it, Chuck? But still, Mr. Bass said not to doubt. That's the most important thing of all, he said — not to doubt."

Now at last they had descended from the mountainous place to the flat land again, and were once more within sight of the low, mounded shapes of the little city. David smiled to see how impatient the little Wise Men were to display their Rolls of Wisdom.

"We will read to you *all* our thoughts," burst out Oru eagerly, bounding up beside them all at once. And he sounded as if that would be the most wonderful treat possible, both for himself and the two boys.

"Well, perhaps not *all* of them," said David doubtfully. "Could you maybe begin at a spot where you feel you're really getting onto the track of the mystery? You see, if you begin *way* back, we won't have time to figure what to do. We have hardly any time left."

Mebe and Oru, trotting along beside them, gazed at each other sadly. You could see how half the fun was being taken out of their reading — imagine not being allowed to reveal *everything* they'd written down! Every single precious word!

"Where must we begin, then?" pondered Mebe, and now the two little men dropped behind again, chattering and arguing and waving their hands about in tremendous disagreement as to the best place to start.

CHAPTER 14

The Cracking of a Shell

WITHIN the city, there was another great commotion at the sight of these two weird, un-Mushroomlike people, but Ta waved back the Basidiumites and explained as he strode along that the two guests were there only to do good. They had come to deliver them all from death. Everything would be all right! Ta cried to his people. And Chuck and David looked at each other and began to wonder what would happen to the two of them if everything turned out *not* to be all right.

At the door of Ta's abode — igloo-shaped like the other houses, but much larger — servants opened the door wide and the boys were ushered into a long, low, round-ceilinged room. On the walls, sconces with flames burning in them glowed on all sides. On the floor were spread what seemed to be dried, fernlike fronds that gave

118

off a faint perfume. Seats were ranged all about the room and these were spread with soft coverings. Everything was palely colored, and all sounds were hushed. There was nothing harsh or rude or violent here, and if Ta and Mebe and Oru had not had such serious faces, thinking of the fate of their people, you could imagine what a happy, untroubled life it might be on Basidium. No traffic, no factories, no hustle and bustle, no war, supposed David. And he tried to think of the earth's being like this, but it was quite beyond him.

Now Ta seated himself with great dignity on a higher, broader seat than the others. He waved the two boys graciously to low seats on either side of, and facing him. Mebe and Oru had gone into another room and presently returned, each bearing big rolls of what seemed to be parchment. But as they unwound them David saw that it was like the substance their robes were made of, but thicker and not transparent.

And then — David's heart sank in despair as Mebe, standing up straight and proud before his king, began to read in a singsong voice from the very beginning of his roll. For it seemed to be a complete history of their food! How pleased he

119

sounded as he read it. You could imagine with what loving care he had put down every word and how *thoroughly* he was enjoying this chance to read aloud his masterpiece!

David took a furtive look at Chuck. Chuck had his chin in his hands, his elbows were on his knees, his eyes were closed, but it was impossible to tell whether he was asleep or not. Now David looked at Ta in desperation, for he could make out, even upside down, that Chuck's wrist watch said half-past three. They had exactly half an hour more, and time here on Basidium, for some reason or other, seemed to go unbelievably fast!

Ta must have seen that desperate look, for all at once he held up his hand.

"Cease!" he commanded. "These are words — words! They mean nothing — they give us no help. Get on to where you make some mention of the magic plant."

But poor little Mebe seemed to go to pieces. He scrambled through his enormous roll like a terri-fied mouse, peered up and down its length with a miserable expression, but seemed to find nothing further that would have been worth reading. He gave several soft, apologetic squeaks, then began quietly tying up his manuscript.

"Continue, Oru!" demanded Ta, pointing a finger at the trembling Oru. So now the other little man commenced.

On and on he droned, gathering happiness from the sound of his own words as he went along. But as he read, David's heart sank even lower. For Oru's scroll turned out to be a history of the sicknesses of the Mushroom People. First they had been taken ill with this, and then with that. Children were apt to suffer from certain illnesses, and grownups from certain other illnesses. And all this was gone into *most* carefully. But none of it shed any light on, or had anything at all to do with, the results of *not* eating the plant which grew up in the Place of the Hidden Water. Indeed there was not a word about the magic plant.

David lowered his head and rested his forehead on his hand. It's no use, he said to himself in despair. They were defeated. There wasn't a thing they could do now. Suddenly Ta got up from his seat and began walking violently up and down the room. And the beautiful stones of his necklace clicked together as he grasped it in his hand, his fingers opening and closing with anger and impatience.

"Silence!" he cried. "Silence! We have no more

121

time. We must talk, we must think, otherwise we are finished!"

Both Wise Men looked at each other, their thin, long hands to their throats. Now the room was absolutely silent except for the sounds Ta's feet made on the dried branches as he paced furiously up and down. And when he glanced at his Wise Men they gazed sorrowfully back at him. They seemed to be saying, without words, that they knew they were defeated.

Suddenly Chuck sighed.

"Well," he said resignedly, "I don't know about the rest of you, but I'm starved." And with that he reached into his pocket and drew out two hard-boiled eggs, handing one graciously to Ta and the other to Mebe. Then he took three more out of his other pocket, gave one to Oru and one to David, and began cracking the shell of the last one on the arm of Ta's chair. "Just brought them along in case we got hungry," Chuck explained. "Never can tell — I'm always getting hungry."

Ta and Mebe and Oru stared at him in utter astonishment, then down at these smooth stones they had been given. What *were* they? their faces said. Chuck gravely peeled off bits of

122

shell, then bit into the smooth white part. "Good," he said, his mouth full. "Try it." He chewed away placidly, looking around as if he were saying: So we've failed — what's to be done? What's the use of being in the dumps about it? And David watched him dismally while Ta and his Wise Men turned their eggs over and over in silent wonderment.

But all at once David saw Chuck stop chewing and stare at his half-bitten egg and then up, his eyes wide and startled.

"Dave!" he yelled, and he jumped from his seat so abruptly that Mebe and Oru almost dropped their eggs. "THE SMELL! THE SMELL! THIS IS IT!" And he came over and shoved his egg under David's nose, then under Ta's and Mebe's and Oru's.

For a moment there was nothing but excited shouts and exclamations.

"It's sulfur!" shouted David. "My mom told me. It's sulfur in the yolk of the egg. That's *it*, Chuck — *the smell up there!* Those are *sulfur* springs! It's sulfur the Mushroom People have to have. Just a little, just a *trace* maybe, but they *have* to have it!"

Then while Chuck was showing Ta and his

Wise Men how to crack the shells of their eggs, and urging them to try a bite or two, David thought fast. Mrs. Pennyfeather! he said to himself.

"Chuck," he announced, "I've decided. We may not get back to earth on time — we may hit the barren wastes of the Tibetan Plateau, or we may go zinging on out into space, but we've *got* to get Mrs. Pennyfeather and explain to Ta what she can do for his people. Come on," he ordered. "We must go at once. You must know, Great Ta, that we have a hen — that is, a fowl — a bird — well, then, a *thing*, a living thing that you don't have here. It lays kind of round objects that look like stones to you. But they're not stones. We call them eggs. And you must keep this living thing we'll give you, and you must put her eggs into water and cook them till they're like this — just as you see them now, firm on the inside. Come! We must hurry!"

So now all of them, Ta and Mebe and Oru and the boys, rushed out of Ta's dwelling and away toward the space ship as fast as their legs would go. When at last they came to it, glimmering in the soft earthlight that drifted through the mist, Chuck quickly boosted David up to the door. He clambered over the entranceway and poised there, his heart pounding for fear Mrs. Pennyfeather might have gotten out and run away. But there she was, that good, faithful hen, fast asleep on Chuck's seat with her head under her wing!

"Come on, Mrs. Pennyfeather," said David, lifting her up gently, "you've got work to do." And then he stared at where she had been sitting, for there were two nice white newly laid eggs. "Here, Chuck, take her," he called down. Then he carefully dropped the eggs, one at a time, into Chuck's hands after Chuck had handed on Mrs. Pennyfeather to the astonished Ta.

Now for the sack of chicken feed, David said to himself. This was going to be a tough one. There it sat upright on top of the oxygen urn, so now David reached down as far as he could, grasped the top of the sack — and pulled! What a weight it was! But in a moment he was able to get his other hand on it, and then he gave a great, final tug and had it onto Chuck's seat. He pushed it through the doorway and heard it go — thunk! — onto the ground below.

"There's your chicken feed," he grinned. But all Mebe and Oru could do was to stare at Mrs.

Pennyfeather as she sat quietly in the arms of the dignified Ta. And it was amazing, thought David, how even with an unknown creature from another planet in his grasp, the Great Ta did not lose his kingly majesty.

"You must take care of her, Great Ta, and be good to her," David said. "She won't hurt you. She's a very nice hen. And every morning, every Time of New Light, she'll give you the white stones."

"Quark," said Mrs. Pennyfeather, as though agreeing, and she peered up at Ta with one round, orange eye.

"And you must understand, sir," said Chucky firmly and seriously, "that you must put the eggs into *cold* water."

"*Cold* water — you hear, simple ones?" Ta said sternly to Mebe and Oru. "Listen well to what is told you!"

"And you must put the water, with the eggs in it, over fire, and get the water hot until it makes bubbles. Let the bubbles keep going for a pretty good while — quite a while, otherwise the eggs will be soft on the inside and you wouldn't like them that way — I don't *think*." Now he gave the freshly laid eggs to Mebe, who tucked them away under his robes into an inside pocket. "Now you must taste the eggs I gave you first, to see how these new ones must be when they are cooked in the hot water."

So Mebe and Oru, who had kept their eggs clutched in their hands while bounding along on the way to the space ship, began to peel off the shells. Then, with scared faces, they gingerly — gingerly — took small bites. They chewed. Then they came to the yolk, and their faces lighted.

"Yes," said little Oru wonderingly, "it is good. It is even — a little like the plant at the Place of the Hidden Water. The feel of it in my mouth is like our plant, though drier — much drier. *And it has the good smell* — that is — the *magic* smell!"

"Don't forget the feed for our hen," warned David, from up in the space ship. "You must give her the little seeds you will find in that bag down there. You must give her a handful every morning, and I think the sack will last until the Time of New Growth — at least, I hope so," he finished, beginning to worry a bit. "But, of course, she can eat worms too, and maybe some of the mossy stuff. Surely worms would love this damp earth."

"And Dave," cried Chuck, a big grin suddenly

127

spreading over his face, "why couldn't Ta or the Wise Men throw one or two handfuls of grain around? Then it'll grow and Mrs. Pennyfeather will always have new grain coming along." David stared at him thoughtfully.

"Yes, why not?" he said at last. "I remember Dad saying it has to be the whole grain, not the split ones. Explain to Ta, will you, Chuck?"

So Chuck slowly and carefully explained about planting some of the whole grains of corn and wheat, about letting the new plants grow until they had ears of grain on them, about parching the grains to feed Mrs. Pennyfeather, and saving some to plant again. Ta listened intently. He asked to be explained to once more, then nodded and repeated it all, and you had a firm feeling that he absolutely understood. If Ta lived on earth, thought David, he would probably be as remarkable there as he was on Basidium.

"Now we must go," finished Chuck, taking a look at his watch. "It's five minutes of four, which means we've got to start off right away. And you must stand back, please," he added, motioning to Ta and Mebe and Oru. "The noise and flame are huge — you will be frightened because you've

128

never seen or heard anything like this before."

"Away with you!" ordered Ta to his Wise Men. He gave Mrs. Pennyfeather into the arms of the trembling Mebe, and Oru stood by his side staring at that good hen with wonder and disbelief written all over his funny little face. Then, watching the Wise Men, taking one last look at them before the space ship should shoot off into the heavens again, David suddenly blinked and rubbed his eyes — and blinked again. Could it be — surely not! Mebe and Oru, it seemed to David, were already starting to turn a faint green! But it must be that he just imagined they were because he had taken it for granted the eggs would work. Yet, as he steadily watched the little men, he had to admit to himself that they were becoming a clear, pale, but quite distinct green. And as they had eaten only a bit of the yolk — for they were holding the rest of the eggs untouched in their hands — it must be true what he had said in Ta's house: that each Basidiumite needed only a trace of sulfur now and then to keep well.

Ta gave an imperious, dismissing wave of his hand and Mebe and Oru scuttled away. Then he stepped forward and, still with kingly gravity, boosted Chuck up into the door of the space ship.

Next he handed up to them their bags of food, and then stood smiling at the two boys, who peered down at him together. "You must have seen," he said, "how the good green has already begun to come back to my two worthless ones. A pity it could not have been bestowed on those more worthy of it."

"Then it was true!" cried Chuck. "I thought I was dreaming."

"Me too!" exclaimed David, giving Chuck a punch out of sheer happiness at the proven success of their mission. "But we weren't dreaming, Chuck. We all saw the green!"

"I have given you no sign of my thanks," Ta went on. "And I have great thanks. There are not many of us here in this land, and we shall need, each of us, only a very little of the heart of the magic stones. What can I give you to show my thanks?"

David looked at Chuck, and they grinned at each other.

"If you please, great Ta," said David, "we wish that you would spare the lives of your two Wise Men."

"Ho!" cried Ta. "Why should you wish the lives of those two insignificant creatures spared? You heard the gabble they have inscribed in their Rolls of Wisdom. Did it help you?"

"No," admitted Chuck, "it didn't. But all the same, we like your little Wise Men. In fact, for some reason, we like them very much!"

"Well, I will tell you a secret," replied Ta, and he looked up at them with a twinkle in his eye. "I, too, am fond of them — very, very fond indeed. And I am happy to have an excuse for saving their lives, foolish though they are. Therefore your wish is granted. But take this also." And now, to the boys' amazement, Ta drew from around his neck the beautiful necklace of stones and flung it up to them — and as it came slithering and swerving upward through the green air, it seemed almost like something alive. "You must divide the stones between you," said Ta, "and because of them, you will always remember me and will know how great are my thanks to you. Those stones were taken from our Sacred Hall in the depths of the mountains, and are given only to the kings of our people."

Chuck and David had never received a gift from a king, so Chuck silently, unable to say a word, rolled up the necklace and stored it away carefully in an inner pocket.

"You are generous, Great Ta. We'll keep the necklace always and we'll divide it absolutely evenly, won't we, Chuck? Now we have to leave. You must stand away, sir —"

"I am not afraid," answered Ta, looking the space ship up and down with a cool eye. "I have never been afraid of anything. But the flame might burn, and I have much to tell my people." Now he started to turn away, but all at once his eye caught something. "What is this?" he cried. And he strode over, picked up something, and held it up to the boys.

"The canning jar!" shouted David, knocking his head with his fist. "Forgotten again! I have a horrible feeling Mr. Bass'll never get it. It's doomed, that canning bottle is." Ta had picked up the lid and was trying to push it onto the top of the jar.

"No, turn it, sir, *turn* it on," called down Chuck. And so, without arguing or questioning or fumbling, Ta turned, and in a trice the lid was tight on and the bottle had been tossed up into David's outstretched, eager hands.

Then Ta lifted his arm, and the boys waved good-by. They closed and bolted the door and strapped themselves in their seats, and David got out his slip of paper to set the controls according to Mr. Bass's directions.

"Time, Chuck?"

"Four — on the nose."

"O.K.," answered David with a sudden tightness in his throat to think that now the last part of their great adventure was beginning, "let's go!"

And he pressed the button and pulled back the lever. There was a frightful roar and a huge flare of red and they were flung backward in their seats with their hearts jumping in their chests. Then at last the smooth motion of the ship under them told them that once more they were on their way out into space, exactly on time with not a moment to spare.

When he got his wits together again, Chuck crawled back and turned on the oxygen urn.

CHAPTER 15

Two Dollars for Adults
and Fifty Cents for Children

"CHUCK," said David after a little, "we made it, didn't we? Mission accomplished!"

"Golly, yes — mission accomplished!" repeated Chuck with quiet satisfaction, and they went through the complicated motions of a secret handshake they had. "But it's kind of lonesome without Mrs. Pennyfeather. I got used to having her in my lap on the way here. She was a nice hen, didn't give any trouble or anything."

"Yes," sighed David, "she was an awfully good hen. I'll miss her a lot. She was such a comfortable sort of bird, not stuck up and temperamental like John. I hope we did the right thing leaving her there. But what else could we have done?"

"Not a thing! Don't begin worrying, not before you have to. We can't go back. Besides, you wouldn't *want* to — that is, to get her. What would the Mushroom People do without her? Say, you know a funny thing, Dave?"

"Well, sort of — you mean about Mr. Bass running after us to be sure we took a mascot?" Chuck nodded, and he narrowed up his eyes.

"I just don't understand it! Do you suppose he *knew*, somehow? But how did he guess we'd take a hen, of all things, the one creature we'd have to have. He didn't even know you *had* a hen!"

But now David frowned and stared off through the window, started to speak, and then was silent again. Finally he made up his mind.

"The only thing that bothers me is, we *should* have taken John and the children."

At this, Chuck began frowning as well, and you could see that he too was beginning to think it would have been a much more satisfactory business if only John and the young chickens had been brought with them. After all, Mrs. Penny-feather might be lonely and begin to pine — and then who could tell what kind of weather Basidium might have, with what disastrous effects on the next crop of sulfur plants? Still, on Basidium, where time passed quickly, the Time of New Growth would soon be round again.

"Well," he said after a bit, "how could we have managed all that chicken feed, Dave? We couldn't have — we just about busted our buttons getting that one sack into the ship." David nodded gravely.

"I know. I've thought of that. All the same, it just seems like —" Then he turned to Chuck and grinned. "It just seems like there's only one answer. We've got to go back." Chuck's eyes widened, and then he slapped his knee.

"But why not, Dave? *Why not?* What's there to stop us from going every night if we like? What's to stop us from going at midnight one night, skipping a night, and then going back home at four o'clock the morning after? *You* know — I mean staying twenty-six hours instead of two? Or a *week*, as long as we started back at exactly four in the morning, like Mr. Bass said?"

This was so staggering an idea that for a minute or two David couldn't answer.

"Why not?" he breathed. "*Why not?* And maybe take Cap'n Tom and Mr. Bass, and then my mother and father — and yours too when they get back from their trip. Then Cap'n Tom'd know you weren't telling a whopper, if he *did* think that. Of course, we couldn't take 'em all at once. The ship's too small. I think we should bring Mr. Bass first — oh, absolutely Mr. Bass first, with Cap'n Tom. Then the rest. That way, we could take the chickens along too, because we'd have plenty of people to help with the sacks of feed."

"Hoora-ay!" shouted Chuck, and he looked as if he'd have jumped up and down if he hadn't been strapped to his seat. "That'll be a lot more stupendous than this trip's been!" But at that David shook his head.

"Not for me it won't," he said firmly. "Nothing could be more stupendous than this trip, because this was the first. There'll never be another like this."

"Well, anyway," said Chuck airily, "what's to stop us from taking *anyone* — I mean, after we've shown our families around over Basidium and given them a nice little taste of space travel — what's to stop us from taking one or two scientists along? You know, jet experts and important astronomers and geologists, and all like that?"

At these words the strangest thing happened to David. At first, right after Chuck had spoken, he felt tremendously excited. Yes — just think

137

of making some grownup's eyes bulge with wonder at all he and Chuck had to show, some astronomer who would have sworn the only satellite of earth was the moon. Think of getting the better of all those grownups who always said nobody would ever land on the moon. Think of that!

And yet, the odd part was that, after his first thrill of excitement, he didn't *like* to think of taking just anyone. It made him feel horribly depressed and unhappy to think of a whole lot of outsiders tramping over Basidium, frightening those gentle little people who were so much like children. Like children, that is, except Ta, who was not like a child at all, who could have faced anyone on earth, David felt, without flickering an eyelash. No, he didn't want to tell the world about Basidium. For he knew, deep down inside, that he didn't want to run the risk of causing any change there.

Those people were happy except during times when nature acted up and made heat waves. There were no automobiles, no clanging stop-and-go signals, no factories, nor roaring trains. There were no wars, and he did not want to be the cause of making it possible for there to be one. The Basidiumites had their own ways. What if he and

Chuck changed all that and the Mushroom People were no longer happy, no longer contented with what they had?

The idea was so terrible to him that he gave a shudder. Then he looked at Chuck, who was waiting for him to answer — because, after all, it had been he, David, who had started all this, the wonderful flight to the Mushroom Planet.

"No, Chuck," David said after a second or two, in which all this had raced through his head. "No — I think it'd be awful to tell people about Basidium, and to take just anybody there. How do we know what they'd want to do? Why, I'll bet they'd start geological expeditions there, and Basidium'd get all dug up. Then after a while there'd be sightseeing tours, and then hot-dog stands and there'd be pop bottles and paper bags thrown around. And the poor little Basidiumites would be stared at, and people would poke them and point to them and try to get in their houses and maybe want to take some of them back to earth to put them on exhibition, and Ta would be angry and hate us. Why, just *think*," shouted David, getting more and more worked up the more he imagined how it would all turn out, "it'd be *terrible!* Can't you see we've got to keep it a secret?"

139

Chuck looked as if he'd been squashed flat. But after a while he sighed.

"I guess you're right," he said finally. "It would be awful — I mean, thinking about Basidium the way it is now, so quiet and peaceful. O' course, I like hot dogs and soda pop and ball games and sight-seeing and all like that. But Ta would have a fit. No, I guess we can't tell people. But how about Grandpop and your folks? You mean we can't even take *them*?"

"I don't see why not. I think they'd understand. Still, maybe it's up to Mr. Bass. Yes, I think really it's up to him. We've got to take him just as soon as possible, along with John and the other chickens and some more feed. Then we'll ask him."

So the matter was settled, at least to David's satisfaction. But you could see how Chuck still longed for sight-seeing tours to Basidium with tickets two dollars for adults and fifty cents for children. Now the boys were quiet for a little, thinking, each to himself, how strange it would be to reach home again, to walk once more upon their own earth — a planet teeming with such complicated affairs as the little Basidiumites could never even dream of.

Then David, thinking of home, suddenly gave

140

a quick, sidelong, rather guilty glance at Chuck.

"Chuck," he began in a peculiar voice. "Chuck, there's something I forgot to tell you. Did you listen to the radio last night?"

"Nope — I didn't. Too busy getting out my winter clothes."

"Well, the newscaster was giving out storm warnings." Chuck turned slowly and studied David.

"Giving out storm warnings for *when?*" he demanded in an ominous tone.

"Now calm down, Chuck. It's nothing. We may even be home before it breaks. He just said it'd hit early this morning sometime, and he was warning the fishermen to put out extra anchors and chain." Chuck was silent for a bit, then he slowly shook his head.

"I don't get it," he said. "I don't get it at all. If Mr. Bass knows so many other things, how come he didn't know —"

"Oh, who's worrying now?" interrupted David just a little too quickly. "You always call me the old worrier! What I say is: Mr. Bass told us not to doubt. He promised us that everything would turn out all right. So let's take it easy, Chuck, and just not worry about getting home safe. Mr. Bass

141

wouldn't have sent us if he'd thought we were going to run into danger. I say we're going to be all right. We've come this far, haven't we? We've accomplished our mission, haven't we?"

"Yep," agreed Chuck, seeming to take heart a little. "That's so, and then we're going so fast that for us the storm won't last very long." He thought for a bit and then he laughed softly to himself. "You know," he said, "I just can't *wait* to see Grandpop's face when we tell him all that's happened — and your mom's face, too. If she thought it was all going to be a dream —" But at this minute Chuck had to give an enormous yawn, so big he looked as if he'd never get his mouth closed again. Then he rubbed his watering eyes.

Yes, thought David, speaking of dreams, he himself was beginning to feel pretty drowsy. What with the smoothness of the ship's motion and the monotonous little peep-peeping of the oxygen urn, and what with not getting all his sleep and then having so many adventures and climbing up to the Place of the Hidden Water and back down again, and having to think so hard, he was about done. He yawned hugely.

"Ay — yow! Are you woozy, Chuck?" But there was no answer. For Chuck's head had fallen forward on his chest and he was fast asleep.

Well, David said to himself, guess I'd better check my controls again, just to be sure. But he was about to reach into his pocket and get out his wallet when it occurred to him that it would be much too much trouble to check them all over again. He knew they were right. He was absolutely sure. And he thought he'd close his eyes just for a moment to see how good it would feel — awfully good — aw-fully good —

CHAPTER 16

Into the Storm

THE WATCH on Chuck's wrist had ticked away for an hour and three quarters, and Mr. Bass's remarkable little mechanism had shut off the rocket motor and turned the ship tail down toward the earth in free fall before the boys opened their eyes again. In a few minutes they would be home.

They stretched, and when they looked up they gasped. For what a wonder met their eyes! Directly above them pulsed the crowding, billion suns of the Milky Way — but never had the boys seen such a Milky Way as this: a broad, majestic cloud of light that reached right across the sky from one side to the other, and so beautiful and seemingly so close that they held their breaths to watch. It's like a tremendous river of suns, said David to himself. And he tried to think of how those crowding suns are part of the galaxy in which we live in our tiny solar system, and that there are other galaxies, other vast clus-

144

terings of thousands of millions of suns, out beyond our own! But it was too much to hold in his mind. The marvel of that luminous arc overhead, set with its great constellations, was enough.

After a little the boys looked down. There beneath them, nearer and nearer, loomed the earth — but such an earth as they had never dreamed of, such an earth as no other boys, except in their dreams perhaps, had ever seen in the history of mankind.

It hung in space, appearing to them from this distance (for now they were only a few thousand miles away) a gigantic, glowing globe. And just as David's father had said on that evening when he first read Mr. Bass's little green notice in the paper, they could see both night and day at once.

On the side of the earth where the sun was shining and it was day, drifts of cloud shone glaring white as they reflected the sun. The polar cap too was dazzling, so dazzling that the boys could scarcely look at it with their naked eyes. Extending up from the polar cap a great gray and brown and green continent stretched toward them, cradled in a brilliant blue sea. And on the night side of the world little cities twinkled in tiny groups like nests of diamonds, while all around the earth's curve lay the deep, deep black of space. The sun's rays could never light that, for there was nothing in it, no dust, no gas, nothing which could reflect light.

Far, far off swam the sun, a blazing ball surrounded by its flaming corona, and so terrible in its brilliance, uncurtained by earth's atmosphere, that they could not look at it at all. On the opposite side of the sky, still in sight, hung the round, silvery-shining orb of the moon.

Like a plummet their ship was dropping toward earth straight into that zone of dawn gray which was their own slim segment of the western hemisphere. As the earth swung up closer and they came at last into the layers of earth's atmosphere, there now began to sweep toward them long gusts of wind like eager sinewy fingers. Only a short distance of their journey remained, it being now precisely four minutes of six o'clock.

Then, just as David turned on the rocket motor to lessen the blow of their landing, the ship suddenly gave a tremendous lurch. A flash of lightning ripped the dark sky and the thunder let out its warning voice — high up, crackling, hesitant, then gaining in speed, and deepening, deepen-

146

ing, until at last it rolled upon them, enveloped them, they were lost in it, and its mighty reverberations seemed to split open the very heavens themselves.

Wildly the ship was flung about in the wind, and all at once, like pellets of steel, hail and sleet were dashed against its sides. Now the constellations were blotted out and the wind and the thunder bellowed together. Forks of lightning sprang at them, and in the intervals of its brilliance, they could see how the clouds were boiling and surging on all sides.

But the most fearsome thing of all was the quivering of the space ship. It roared, as though all its force were being pitched against an even greater force, the terrible, rushing wind. It seemed to fight and struggle, and when the wind lessened, on it went, only to start bucking and lurching again.

"I'm scared, Chuck!" cried out David.

"So'm I!"

"We're being swept off our course. If we ever get down, we're going to land bang in the middle of the ocean."

"We'll never make it, Dave. Mr. Bass was wrong. He should never have sent us."

But at mention of Mr. Bass, David determined to get hold of himself. What was the use of being scared? he asked himself sternly. The only thing to do was to try to keep the ship on its course — to keep it on the beam as best he could.

"What time is it, Chuck?" he shouted.

"Six! We're not making time — not by a long shot."

"Hey there, Mr. Bass!" called out David as a kind of feeble joke, though he could scarcely hear his own voice in the uproar. "We're almost home. Keep an eye on us, will you?"

But the only answer was the crash of thunder and the crackle of lightning, like a tough piece of silk being savagely ripped in two. Hail beat against the window as though it were determined to shatter it, to crack it to bits. And just then David decided that, Mr. Bass or no Mr. Bass, it was hard not to be afraid.

"Flashlight, Chuck!" he yelled. "On the instrument panel."

Chuck flashed his beam and David saw with a plunging heart how the needles were being dashed drunkenly from side to side. He tried, after struggling with his pocket flap and his wallet and at last getting out Mr. Bass's paper, to set the controls correctly again — but it seemed quite hopeless.

"We can't make it, Chuck! It's no use!"

But now, it seemed to them, the darkness began to lessen a little. All about them the clouds were becoming a dull gray. The hail and sleet fell off, and the thunder rolled away like a giant's bowling balls, banging and slamming against one another farther and farther down the sky.

Beneath them, as the clouds parted here and there for an instant, they caught glimpses of a gray expanse of ocean, then a dark shore line of jagged, wooded rock. Now even the wind seemed to be giving up its battle, and slowly David felt the knots of fear in his stomach begin to relax.

"It's two minutes after six, Dave," Chuck announced presently in an exhausted voice. "I guess we're going to make it. Either the storm's over or we've beaten it home. Or maybe it's taken a detour. Just think — *we're going to make it,* Dave! Mr. Bass was right."

Down they hurtled, tail first into a bleak and windswept world. There lay the Monterey shore with its huddled cluster of houses, the fishing boats bobbing and dancing on the roughened waters, and dark patches of trees bending under

149

the force of the gale. Away up the coast, storm clouds bore toward them. But beneath them lay the comforting, welcoming stretch of Cap'n Tom's beach.

And there — *could* they be certain? — but how their hearts leaped — was not just the speck of that dark rock upon which they'd climbed to get into their upended ship for the blast-off, but another speck as well! Lonely and infinitely tiny it looked on that gray stretch of sand. And did it move? *Was* there a signal given as though an ant had waved its antennae? The shore line drew closer, seemed to expand — and the speck grew into the little figure of a living being.

"Dave — it's — it's Mr. Bass! He's come down to welcome us. We're home!"

CHAPTER 17

Nothing But a Tinkle in the Wind

Now, as they neared the beach, David speeded up the motor in order to counteract the pull of gravity. The little ship, desperately trying to struggle upward in the direction its nose was pointed and yet drawn inescapably downward by gravity, fairly shuddered in the conflict between these opposing forces. For a second they were poised just above the sand — then David turned off the motor and down they came. They were safe!

Belts were snatched off, the door was wrenched open and there — waving and calling — his long funny gray gardening coat flapping and whipping about his knees just exactly as it had the last time they'd seen him, was Mr. Bass hurrying toward them along the dim beach. And what a broad and happy smile was on his face!

"Mr. Bass! Mr. Bass! We did it! We did every-thing —"

"— and there was a storm, Mr. Bass. But we got through —"

"— and we saved the Basidiumites, Mr. Bass. We took Mrs. Pennyfeather —"

"— she's a chicken, and she was our mascot. Just think, Mr. Bass, if it hadn't been for Mrs. Pennyfeather —"

But surely little Mr. Bass was about to be blown away. Surely that tiny figure, frail as a dried leaf, could not withstand the onslaught of the wild wind a moment longer.

"Come down, boys, come down. Welcome home! Oh, *what* a triumph, a *great* triumph. How proud I am of you — but I knew you would do it. Do come down at once so that we can talk!"

The rock was some distance off, and so, each with his big bag of food, the boys jumped out and tumbled on the sand at Mr. Bass's feet, laughing and gasping. Eagerly he put an arm around each, then joyfully shook their hands. And so beaming was his smile and so proud his eyes that they were made to feel like the first and greatest explorers of all time.

"A triumph!" he exclaimed again. "I had never a moment of doubt, only I regret the storm. That, Chuck and David, I will have to admit, gave me pause for thought. Were you frightened? Oh, I do hope —"

But how strange! For now that it was all over it seemed to the boys to have been the most ter- rifically exciting experience they had had, except landing on Basidium.

"Why, it was nothing, Mr. Bass — just nothing at all! That is, it was — it was —"

"— stupendous!" finished Chuck. "That — and the moment we landed, and the moment we found that Mrs. Pennyfeather's eggs had what the Basidiumites needed, and the moment we —"

"— the moment we met Ta. Remember that, Chuck? And remember how he —"

"— how he gave us his necklace! Oh, Mr. Bass, you must see it — you must —"

But little Mr. Bass put back his head and gave a long, thin, high, airy laugh. He laughed and laughed. Then he laid a hand on the arm of each of them.

"My dear boys," he said, "I have so little time. I had to welcome you, no matter what else hap- pened. But first, before I leave you, I must take with me that bottle of Basidium air. Do you have it?" he asked, and you could see the excitement, the almost boyish excitement, that shone in his great round eyes.

What a *good* thing it was to have that bottle for him, thought David, watching Chuck rustle around in his bag. Yes, there it was! There was the canning bottle full of Basidium air — and in the gray morning light how positively unearthly it looked sitting there on Chuck's hand, for it shone like a jewel of *precisely* Basidium green — that lovely, luminous bluish green that David knew he could never forget no matter how long he lived.

"Ah!" breathed Mr. Bass. He took the bottle in his thin, almost transparent fingers and held it up and gazed at it as though it were a long lost friend. Then — quickly — he unscrewed the lid, took a breath, and popped the lid back on again before you could say Jack Robinson! "Oh my!" he whispered. "That smell — why, it takes me back thousands of years! Would you believe it!"

The boys gasped and stared. *"Thousands* of years, did you say, Mr. Bass?" ventured Chuck, thinking surely he had been mistaken.

154

"Goodness, yes. Why, just one whiff wafted me over the centuries as though they had been nothing." Carefully Mr. Bass tucked the bottle inside his coat and then buttoned the coat up so that the bottle made a funny sort of bulge on his whispy figure. Then he held out a hand to each of them. "Boys," he said very solemnly, "you must get your rest now. And then I should like you to meet me at my house at, let us say, ten o'clock. Yes, I believe ten o'clock would be just right if there is nothing else you must do. Then I can have a full account of your journey with nothing skipped, down to the last detail. And perhaps by then I shall have the results of my analysis of Basidium air. Shall we say ten, then?"

"Yes, Mr. Bass."

"Oh, yes — but Mr. Bass, why do you have to hurry away?" cried David. "Can't we talk now? We're not in the least tired."

"Ah, but you will find you are, David — *very* tired. By six-thirty you will be sound asleep, and you will be sunk deep until at least nine. Meanwhile, I have a great deal to do, oh, a *great* deal! You see, I have an appointment — the most important appointment of my life, and I must be ready."

"When is it, Mr. Bass?" asked Chuck.

"Well," said little Mr. Bass, "I'm not just sure. But it will be soon, of that I am certain. I've thoroughly cleaned my house for the first time in — ah, hm-m-m — well, some weeks, shall we say, and I have most of my papers in order. But there are still quite a few things to be done."

The most important appointment of his life and he wasn't certain when it was to be!

"Are you afraid, Mr. Bass?" asked David, remembering vividly that moment when he had pulled back the stick and pressed the button just before they had set off for Basidium.

"*Afraid?* Dear me, no!" smiled Mr. Bass in surprise. "Why should I be afraid? Well now, Chuck and David, I must hurry. Ten o'clock, then. You won't forget, will you?"

As if they could possibly forget! Away went Mr. Bass, and as he scurried off down the beach, it seemed to the two boys, standing there looking after him, that the fitful wind suddenly rose in force. Did his hurrying feet touch the sand? Now he disappeared round the other side of the big rock, and with Mr. Bass gone, weariness overtook them. Or perhaps they felt their tiredness for the first time. Now that Mr. Bass wasn't there, it

156

seemed to David that an electric current had been shut off.

Battered by the wind, the two boys once more hauled up their heavy bags of food and staggered away across the beach.

"We ought to put the space ship back in the cave, Chuck," shouted David. And yet, at the thought of hauling that big, heavy thing up over the sand, he felt he couldn't make it, even with the help of the carrier, which was still there.

"Can't!" shouted back Chuck. "We'll just have to —" and then the wind died, and there was Chuck shouting furiously into silence. "We'll just have to leave her there for now," he finished in an ordinary voice, looking rather foolish.

"Guess it's far enough back from the wave line," murmured David, turning to look at their ship glimmering silver gray in the early morning light. "Tide's going out, I think. She'll be all right." Now they plugged ahead again in a kind of queer, ominous stillness. Boom! roared the churned-up ocean. Then the wind gathered itself and plunged at the coast again and all the ancient little cypress trees shivered and shook, and the pines joined their voices with the sea's. At the parting of the ways the boys scarcely paused.

"See you later, Dave. I'll be over about a quarter of ten. Got to do some sleeping first."

David climbed tiredly toward his back gate, and when he passed John and Mrs. Pennyfeather's house, he had a funny little feeling of sadness. Just think, he said to himself, Mrs. Pennyfeather was way out in space, 50,000 miles away, on a planet no earthly bird or person had ever seen — except himself and Chuck, and Mr. Bass, in a way. A shiver went through him. Was it the wind?

Then he realized something. Ever since he and Chuck had waked up, they'd been speaking English. He knew that, and he knew that before they'd gone to sleep, after leaving Basidium, they'd still been speaking words that were not English. Now he tried to reach back in his memory for snatches of that strange, faraway tongue. How had he and Chuck spoken to Ta and his two Wise Men? What was the word, for instance, for "ground" or for "mountain" or for "water"? He hadn't the faintest notion. All that he could recall now was that they had spoken in a kind of singsong way, with the words going up and down as the Chinese speak, and in thin, high-pitched voices.

He stared at the hen house, making an enormous effort to remember just one word. That was all he asked — just to get back one word. But his mind was blank. His memory held nothing but the faroff sound of little high voices like a tinkle of glass in the wind. This was all that was left. Almost — he might never have been on Basidium.

"Oh, but I *was* there!" he exclaimed aloud — and now he started toward the house again. "I *was* there! Chuck and I were there, and we're going back!"

In another ten minutes David had crept in at the door, put all his food away, folded up the big brown bag, slipped out of his clothes and into his pajamas, and was curled in a roll with the blankets pulled up snugly under his chin.

He lay there in his bed listening. Absolute stillness — and then a screen slammed suddenly against the outside of the house. Now it was ripped from its fastenings and sent crashing and banging, helter-skelter, away down the sidewalk, and the house was shaken by the wind as though it were about to be loosed from its foundations. The giant with the bowling balls sent one of them booming across the skies so that the rumble echoed away and away over the mountains. Then the rains came down, slashing and streaking against the windows.

"Basidium —" whispered David. "I want to go back — must go back — right away —"

Then he was asleep, and even when one of those black bowling balls sped across the sky and hit another, square on, right over his roof, he did not move.

PART THREE

A Most Mysterious Disappearance

CHAPTER 18

The Angry Sea

Aʙᴏᴜᴛ nine o'clock that morning—long after Dr. Topman had started off on his round of calls despite the storm — David sat at the breakfast table in the nice warm kitchen telling his mother the whole marvelous story.

There she sat, her cup of coffee cooling unnoticed at her elbow, her toast grown quite cold and soggy.

"And *then* — ?" she would cry. "And what did these enormous mushroom trees look like — I mean, *exactly* what did they look like? And do the people actually make their clothes out of mushrooms? And the merinbun, or whatever he was — was he black or brown? Was he like a dinosaur? Did he have fur?"

"No, but he was kind of like a huge, tremendous sloth —"

163

"And Ta — what did *he* say? And then what did *you* say — and so what did you do *then*? And David, what about their houses — and were there birds — ?" and so on and so on. And she was full of questions about the effect of that damp climate on the Mushroom People, and about time on Basidium (did it seem the same as here?), and about the exact length of the day, and whether the Mushroom People had invented the wheel yet or not, and whether they had beds or lay on the floor, and whether they had stoves, and what they used for pots and pans and dishes, and whether the children seemed kindly treated and well behaved.

"Ah, but then," she reminded herself, "everyone was in the middle of a crisis, and so perhaps you couldn't really judge —"

"Besides being in such an awful hurry," added David, "to get through the city and on up into the mountains." His mother gave a big sigh.

"Well," she said, "in spite of being the parent of a space man who has just returned from a hitherto unknown satellite, I must do the dishes and make the beds. Oh dear," and she looked out of the window at the sodden landscape, "*poor* John and Mrs. Pennyfeather and the children — they'll be so hungry. It's letting up a bit, David. You simply must go out there and —"

"But, Mother!" exclaimed David in stunned surprise, "I just got through telling you how we took Mrs. Pennyfeather to Basidium, and how if it hadn't been for her —"

"There!" cried Mrs. Topman, clapping her hands to her head, "you see what habit does. I clean forgot, just for a moment, about her being your mascot. You *did* take food along for her, I hope?"

"Yes, Mom," replied David in a funny sort of voice, quiet and serious, with all the excitement gone out of it, "we took a whole bag of feed. And by the time the feed's all used up, why then the Time of New Growth will be around again, and she'll have sulfur plants or whatever else she can eat around the sulfur springs."

"Good!" said Mrs. Topman, getting up and beginning to carry the dishes away from the table, "but I do hope Mrs. Pennyfeather can eat sulfur plants — or find something there she likes, though there's no use worrying about it now. Even if she were to — well, you know — a hen can't last forever, and anyway, the important thing, of course, was for the Mushroom People to be saved." She

165

hummed to herself and then went over to the radio. "Wonder what the news is about the storm. I've been thinking about the fishing fleet — the wind and all —" and she lifted her head to listen to it driving across the roof.

But David said nothing. For all at once he had an awful sinking feeling that just maybe, in spite of herself, and in spite of everything she had said and all the questions she had asked, his mother actually believed the whole thing to have been a dream. And maybe, even, she wouldn't have been in the least surprised to find Mrs. Pennyfeather down in the chicken house this very minute.

"Mother," he began, "Mother, tell me — would you be willing to go to Basidium if Mr. Bass didn't mind?" At this, Mrs. Topman looked up and stared at him. "Will you go, Mom? Will you?" Then she smiled, an odd little smile.

"Why yes, of course I'll go, David — but it's rather frightening, isn't it?" Her eyes widened, then her glance wavered and fell away. "Of course we'll go — sometime."

"No, *not* sometime — tonight! You and Mr. Bass, and we can take John and the children and more feed. Then I'd feel better."

166

Oh, but she didn't believe — she didn't believe! He knew that. He could see it in her face. And she had to. He had to *make* her believe in some way — and he was about to put his proof to her step by step, when the newscaster's rich, jovial voice suddenly filled the room.

"— and here's a little item that's been giving us a great deal of amusement in the newsroom. A small boy phoned in a few minutes ago to tell us that this morning, very early, before the storm had gotten well under way but after the big wind had already begun, he looked out of his window and saw a neighbor of his swooped up by the gale and whipped right off into the sky. Up and up he went — so the little boy said — turning this way and that, his coat flapping about his ears, until he finally vanished altogether, a mere speck in the clouds." Over the radio came the deep, hearty, jolly voice of the newscaster, relishing to the fullest this ridiculous story. "Well," he finished, still chuckling, "I guess there's just no telling what's going to happen around here. Some storm!"

Mrs. Topman turned, laughing.

"Isn't that funny?" she said. "Imagine!"

"No," said David. "I don't really think it's

funny," and he turned and went off to his room to think, and the minute he got there, he remembered something.

"The necklace!" he exclaimed aloud. "Chuck's got it — Ta's necklace — that's it!" When Chuck came over, he, David, would take his share of the stones and give them all to his mother — and then she would believe. And what was more, she and Cap'n Tom must come with them when they went to Mr. Bass's for their appointment.

He looked at the clock. He had fifteen minutes before Chuck would arrive, so quickly he got into his rubber boots and raincoat and hurried down to the hen house. Already, in the damp, gray air, the young chickens were out pecking about for their breakfast, and over in one corner of the henyard John stood disconsolately with drooping, dirtied tail feathers. Was it because his wife had left him — or had been so rudely snatched from him — that he looked such a miserably unhappy bird?

Hastily David threw handfuls of grain around, and it was remarkable, he thought, how much more cheerful John became, even though, as he strutted hastily over, he still managed to carry his air of bereaved dignity.

168

Now David went on down toward the end of the cypress hedge. There he'd have a good uninterrupted view of the beach and could reassure himself at once that the space ship, despite having been left out on the sand instead of being stowed carefully away in the cave, was still safe and sound.

But what a terrible sight met his eyes! With a wildly beating heart he searched that curving strip of dark sand, pounded by the huge breakers, for some sign of the ship. But it was gone. There was not a sign of it the whole length and breadth of the beach, at least as far as he could see. Oh, tired as they had been, *why* hadn't they put their ship away? Now he started to run, but even when he got past the row of cypresses and onto the beach itself, there was no space ship. All that was left in its place was a scattering of wood and tin and, far up near the cave, one battered, soaked, torn-up old cushion. The cave itself was dark and damp and cold.

There was no need to wonder what had happened. In the dim light of early morning the roaring tide had come in, clawing and reaching with its strong gray fingers. It had dragged the space ship close and fallen upon it and battered it, picked it up and hammered it on the rocks and the hard sand until there was nothing left but this sad scattering of debris flung far and wide up and down the shore line.

David's eyes blurred as he reached over to pick up a piece of tin. Yes, there were the little holes all around it, where he or Chuck had nailed it onto the long, curving body of the space ship. And over a bit farther he found the little spigot from the oxygen urn almost buried in the sand. His eyes were hot and stinging, but he blinked hard as he turned the spigot over and over in his fingers, then hid it away in his pocket.

It really didn't matter about the ship, he told himself (but all the same, as he stared out over the churning water he knew that, just in this moment, he hated the sea). It really didn't matter, because there wasn't any reason why he and Chuck couldn't build another.

Still, he knew somewhere inside himself that they couldn't. There had been something about that ship, something about the building of it, and about the journey it had taken them on that could never happen again. Someday, when he was a man, he might have another space ship and go on another journey, but it would not be such a journey as this had been, because he would be old then and nothing would be the same!

Ah, but what if Mr. Bass wanted them to go back? What if he asked them to get to work at once and build another ship? There was only one thing left to do now and that was to go to Mr. Bass and tell him the whole thing. Perhaps Mr. Bass would be angry that they had been so careless, for now his oxygen urn and his cylinders were gone, and if they were like his other inventions he could never, never repeat them exactly again. But somehow, thought David, that was one thing you couldn't imagine — Mr. Bass being angry.

He turned and ran up the beach, and when he came to his house, the back door opened and out stepped his mother and Cap'n Tom and Chuck, all ready to start.

"They're coming too, Dave," shouted Chuck. "Is it all right, do you s'pose? I thought it was time they met Mr. Bass."

David came up to them slowly.

"Yes," he said, "it's time they met him. They've got to, Chuck, so they can hear about Basidium from him. Cap'n Tom, did you think Chuck was telling you a whopper this morning?" Cap'n Tom grinned down sideways at Chuck, and Chuck kicked the toe of his shoe once or twice against the side of the porch. "Chuck," exclaimed David urgently, "the necklace! Show it to them — just *show* it to them! Show it to my mom." But now Chuck's face slowly changed and took on an expression of almost frightened surprise.

"Why, Dave, I left it in the space ship. I thought all this time you had it. Don't you remember when we were scrambling around for the bags of food so we could jump out quick and talk to Mr. Bass, the necklace dropped out of my pocket? It landed down on the oxygen urn, and you got out last so I thought maybe you had it." All the urgency had faded from David's face. There was a long moment of utter silence. Then David shoved his hands in his pockets.

"Well," he said in a voice that shook a little, "I *haven't* got it — that's all. The sea's got it. And the sea's got our space ship, too, and we'll never see either of them again." He turned away for a second and bit his lip hard. Then from his pocket he pulled out the spigot of the oxygen urn. "Here's all that's left." Chuck took the little spigot and turned it over and over in his fingers just as David had done on the beach, while Cap'n Tom and Mrs. Topman gazed sadly at the two boys without, apparently, being able to find a word of comfort.

"Gone!" muttered Chuck finally. "Both of them gone. What will Mr. Bass say?" But at this, Cap'n Tom put an arm across Chuck's shoulder.

"There's no reason you can't build another ship, boys. I've had two ships go down under me, but I always got another."

"Yes, but yours weren't space ships, Grandpop," said Chuck in a low voice. "Yours weren't *special* ships with things in them nobody could ever make again. I just almost wish we'd never come back!" At this Cap'n Tom looked stern.

"Seems to me we're getting in the doldrums here, and there's only one cure for that. We'll just heave to and get on over to this Mr. Bass's and see what he's got to tell. Look sharp now, men — we're under way."

But no sooner was everyone settled in the car with Mrs. Topman at the wheel and the first block behind them, than Chuck leaned forward all at once and touched her on the shoulder.

"Let me out, will you, Mrs. Topman?" he said.

173

"There's something I've got to see about — right away." Mrs. Topman drew over to the curb and turned and looked at Chuck in surprise.

"Why, Chuck, what's the matter? Aren't you going to Mr. Bass's with us?" Chuck shook his head and set his lips in a way David knew, and his expression meant he wasn't to be budged.

"Nope, I'm not going," he said. "Got to see about something."

So out he hopped, and nobody asked him any questions because you could tell he didn't *want* to be asked any questions. He looked extremely serious, and the last they saw of him he was going around the corner of David's house very fast.

CHAPTER 19

Like a Leaf in the Sky

F<small>IVE MINUTES</small> later they drew up outside Mr. Bass's house. And what a chaos the storm had made of his garden. As in many other gardens they had passed, leaves and pine needles were everywhere — thick along the paths and sidewalks, in drifts in the gutters, and even pasted flat against windows. Branches were torn down, and a little new tree at the side of Mr. Bass's gate had been entirely uprooted.

Out they got, David leading the way with Cap'n Tom and Mrs. Topman next in single file. David opened the gate and with a quick-beating heart (for now, already, he was beginning to wonder if he ever really *had* seen Mr. Bass at all) scuffed his way along the strewn and littered path.

How quiet everything was now that the storm

175

was over. Mr. Bass's house was so buried in trees that you felt, as you drew near it, as if you were completely shut away from the hustle of the town — and, indeed, you might have been in the middle of a wood. Now a bird piped a single, questioning note, and off somewhere in the underbrush there was a quick rustle as of some small animal running to hide.

But not a sound came from the little house. Not a shred of smoke curled from the chimney. There was not a movement at the windows. Now, curiously fearful, David went up the front steps, held out his hand, hesitated, then doubled his fist over and knocked. His mother and Cap'n Tom stood quietly behind him. But there was no answer.

"Try again," said Cap'n Tom.

So David knocked two more knocks, quite loud. But still — no answer.

"Well," said Mrs. Topman, and she sounded as if she were trying to be perfectly reasonable and ordinary, "that's a funny thing. But he may have gone to do some marketing. Suppose we try round the back. Or maybe he's down cellar."

So they all trooped round to the side of the house, peered into the dark where only the little mushroom heads gleamed palely, and then went

176

round to the back. But there was no answer there either.

"But he asked us *specially* to be here at ten o'clock on the dot!" wailed David.

"Dear!" said Mrs. Topman, and she sounded distinctly annoyed. "I do think he might have left a note."

But suddenly David gave an exclamation and pointed a finger at the window of the back porch.

"I saw that curtain move!" he cried.

So up the back steps they hurried again and once more David knocked. Still — no answer, and at this point Cap'n Tom held up his hand with authority.

"There's more here," he said, "than meets the eye. Wait, and I will go round to larboard and inquire of the natives. Only sensible procedure."

And he was just about to go when the back door opened, and from the dimness inside there peered out an eye.

"Hi," said someone. "You looking for Mr. Bass?" The voice came from rather low down, and it sounded as if it belonged to a person somewhat younger than David.

"Why yes, dear," exclaimed Mrs. Topman eagerly, "as it happens, we are. Have you seen him

177

about?" Now the head of a small boy of about six appeared.

"I did this morning," said he, "but he blew away."

There was a moment of stunned silence.

"*Blew away!*" burst out Cap'n Tom at last. "Great jumpin' Jehosaphat! What was that ye said — blew *away?*"

"Yes, sir," said the little boy respectfully, but in a perfectly matter-of-fact voice. "My mum let me phone the radio station and I told 'em — he blew away. I saw him. I looked out of my window when the wind was really getting strong — and I saw Mr. Bass go up in the air like a leaf in the sky —" here the little boy made an upward, fluttering movement of his hand — "and that was the last of him. After it stopped raining, I came over here to look for him. I looked in his planta —— in his observ-tory, and in the closets, and under the bed, and behind the curtains, and down in the cellar, and *everywhere* — but he's gone. He blew away all right."

There was another moment of profound silence.

"Are you sure this is true?" asked Cap'n Tom sternly after a bit.

"Yes, sir," said the little boy. "My mum just laughed, but she said I could phone anyway. She thinks Mr. Bass is going to come back. But he won't."

"Did she say, too, that you might have been dreaming?" asked Mrs. Topman anxiously.

"Yes," said the little boy.

"I was afraid of that," said Mrs. Topman, "and of course you weren't. Did you like Mr. Bass a lot?"

"Oh, yes — he was wonderful! You should see the things he made for me. You couldn't ever buy 'em at a store. Stores wouldn't *think* of things like Mr. Bass could make."

"And will you be sad — that is," said Mrs. Topman hastily, "will you miss Mr. Bass?"

"Why *sure*," said the little boy, as if anybody with a lick of sense would know that. "O' *course* I'll miss him! But he's gone on an adventure and it'll be fun. He'll have a wonderful time! And he always *said* he'd blow away *sometime*, because he's a spore person. Mr. Bass told me that."

Everybody stood around in a circle and just looked at the little boy, because they couldn't think of a single thing to say. But then all at once:

"Jim-mm-eee!" came a voice from over in the next garden.

"There's my mum," he said, and quick as a rabbit he scuttled off down the stairs and away through the bushes. After he was gone not a leaf moved, not a bird piped — there wasn't a sound anywhere.

"*Well!*" said Cap'n Tom. "A *spore person!* B' the great white whale! Only thing to do now is to have a look around. Might find something. Stands to reason we'll find something. Have an idea Mr. Bass wouldn't mind."

So in they went, even though David felt he could not bear to go into that empty little house now that Mr. Bass was gone. *Blown away!* Of course, it was just like him — it seemed to David that that was just exactly how Mr. Bass would go somewhere, but not *now*. Not today, of all days. Why would he have let himself be blown away just when he should have been waiting to hear how everything had turned out?

"He's got to be here, Mom. He's got to be somewhere."

But he wasn't.

He wasn't in the closet, nor under the bed, nor

in the kitchen, nor under the sofa, nor behind the curtains, nor down cellar, nor up in the observatory. He just wasn't anywhere.

"By golly," they heard Cap'n Tom chuckle to himself out in the little kitchen. "Neat and clean and snug as a ship's galley. All the pots and pans shining, and all the cutlery in place —"

"Oh dear," said Mrs. Topman, coming away from peeking into Mr. Bass's bedroom, "I wonder if we should take the liberty of coming into someone else's house and looking into all the corners. It seems impolite, somehow —" But when she saw the steps leading to the observatory, she seemed suddenly overcome with the delight of exploring. "Though of course," she said to David, who had already gone aloft and was looking down at her, "on the other hand, if Mr. Bass is really gone —" And up she climbed with Cap'n Tom crowding after.

In the observatory, which they filled to the walls (Cap'n Tom being, after all, quite a large man), they stared all around at Mr. Bass's enormous collection of books, his instruments of celestial exploration, and the curious domed, ridged ceiling above them. And did the others feel as he himself felt, wondered David, something extraordinary here in Mr. Bass's little house, something *waiting?*

"Oh, it's no use, David, I'm afraid," said Mrs. Topman at last in a low voice, as though she didn't want to be overheard. "We might just as well give up and go home. We'll have to be content with biding our time until Mr. Bass chooses to appear again."

But David did not follow when the other two filed down the steps.

"Where are you, Mr. Bass?" he asked the eerie, gray morning stillness that filled the small room. "Where have you gone? Please come back!"

And then — as if in answer, there came a muffled exclamation from the depths of Mr. Bass's house, and the sound of scurrying feet. In less than a breath, David was down the observatory steps and into the living room, while down cellar could be heard the happy boom of Cap'n Tom's voice and a sharp cry of excitement from Mrs. Topman.

"Wha-at!" yelled David at the top of his lungs on his way round to the cellar door. "What is it? *Wait! Wait for me!"*

CHAPTER 20

I, Tyco Bass

In the soft, clear radiance of the cellar light, in the midst of Mr. Bass's jungle of assorted contraptions, stood Cap'n Tom with a long, legal-looking envelope in his hand.

"A letter, David, a letter!" he shouted, as David rushed in at the door. "By jings, it's a letter from — looks like — Ly-co M. — or no, *Tyco* M. Bass. And it's for you boys. Says here: 'To Masters David Topman and Charles Masterson,' and it's got your address underneath, David, and it's all stamped and ready to mail. Found it here on the workbench, under a paperweight, along with the bills for the gas and light and water. Funny place for bills, I'd say — down cellar." David reached out and took the letter and his eyes were huge.

"Mr. Bass never did what anyone expected him

183

to, I guess," and with trembling fingers he turned the envelope over and over, and at last, very deliberately, with his tongue in the corner of his mouth, he tore open one end and drew forth two folded sheets of paper. These he flattened, and he was beginning to read them to himself when Mrs. Topman all at once gave an exclamation of impatience.

"Goodness to gracious, child!" she cried. "Read out, read out, so we can all hear!"

And at that, David finally read out.

"'Dear Chuck and David,'" he began, his voice tense and shaking, "'I have a feeling at this moment too strong to be ignored that my time here on earth has come to an end. The hour for my appointment has arrived, and though I cannot have my visit with you, at least I can tell you of some plans I have made.

"'You boys have thought, no doubt, that because of my energy and great interest in so many different things, I am no older than the average grandfather. But, as I told you, the Mushroom People live quickly. And for a descendant of the Mushroom People, I am very, very old indeed — so old that you might have trouble in believing me if you knew my secret.

" 'I had a feeling even before I met you on the beach this morning that the mission upon which I had sent you was triumphantly completed. I am eternally grateful to you. Now that I know my people are safe — because of you — I can draw my earthly affairs to a close and prepare myself to go elsewhere.

" 'I do not know where I shall go — certainly not to Basidium, for I finished that phase of my existence many centuries ago. No, my next life will be on some other planet, though where that planet lies in all the billions of starry galaxies that surround this little sphere, I have no idea. But I am not sad to be going, nor frightened of what may lie ahead of me. Indeed, I look forward to this new adventure with joy.

" 'Because of your courage and willingness to do what was asked of you, Chuck and David, in spite of the many obstacles that lay in your path (not to speak of the thousands of miles it was necessary for you to travel through space), I wish to express my gratitude to you in a way that I believe will bring you lasting pleasure.

" 'Aside from a cousin by the name of Theodosius Bass, who is a great wanderer, loves to travel light, and who has never cared to be troubled with properties, I have no kith or kin to whom to leave my possessions. Therefore:

" 'I, Tyco M. Bass, being of sound mind, do herewith make my last will and testament, that the aforementioned David Topman and Chuck Masterson, of Pacific Grove, California, shall be my assignees and heirs. They are to inherit my full property, which consists of the land at 5 Thallo Street, Pacific Grove, California, and all of the possessions contained within this property and within this house, to be theirs, jointly, for the rest of their natural lives. The inheritance is to be turned over, thereafter, to the city of Pacific Grove.

" 'It is my wish (though they may do as they think best) that my house and my property be used as the headquarters and meeting place of a Society, under their management, of Young Astronomers and Students of Space Travel. There shall be a President, chosen by them: an adult of scientific, yet humorous and imaginative, turn of mind.

" 'The members of the Society shall be chosen also by Masters Chuck and David, after due consideration as to their fitness for membership, and interest in the subjects of astronomy and space

186

travel. They should be young people who will use carefully the books and instruments of celestial exploration which I am leaving for their enjoyment.

" 'From the members of the Society, a number shall be selected by majority vote to undertake the various duties that will be necessary, under the guidance of the President.

" 'On the separate sheet of paper enclosed here, you will find, Chuck and David, the combination of a small wall safe which is in the observatory. In this safe I should like you to keep a certain filter of which I told you, and which is there now. Also, I believe it would be well to keep your necklace there. Both these objects relate to a matter which should be kept an absolute SECRET — a secret *never* to go beyond the circle of your immediate family! Even the members of your Society are not to be a party to this affair, for the time has not yet come when it will be safe and proper for these things to be known. Both of you have thought this matter over very carefully, and the conclusions you came to were the right ones.

" 'I am sorry that I have not time to tell you the results of my analysis of that canning bottle of

Basidium air. I can only say that the results were fascinating — fascinating beyond my wildest imagination. I had the choice of writing out this will, or of writing a long scientific paper, and I felt that this was the more urgent.

" 'Good-by, my dear friends. I am happy that we have met and it is my great hope that we shall meet again in the distant future. I see no reason why we shouldn't.

" 'Yours most sincerely,
(Signed) *Tyco M. Bass*' "

After this incredible document had been read, everybody just stood and stared at everybody else. David was dazed and speechless. Mrs. Topman finally remarked that she wished she could sit down somewhere. But Cap'n Tom, having been faced with many and many a breath-taking situation in his lifetime, took hold of this new turn of events with his usual steadiness and calm.

"Is that the paper with the combination to the safe on it, David?"

"Yes," said David, staring at it, then staring at Mr. Bass's letter in wonder.

"Then stow it away all safe in your wallet, boy, and get it memorized as soon as possible. Next, we must see to it that all this is brought up before my lawyer — all matters pertaining immediately to the will, that is, but not to your secret, of course. The boundaries of Mr. Bass's property will have to be legally determined and the whole thing gone into quite thoroughly."

"Cap'n Tom, what do you suppose your lawyer will *say?*" Cap'n Tom chuckled.

"If he says anything at all, I shall simply remind him that 'There are more things in heaven and earth, Horatio, than are dreamt of in your philosophy.' "

"I *wish* Chuck was here!"

Now David's eye lit on the canning bottle, plain glass-colored as it had been before it went to Basidium, sitting on Mr. Bass's work bench with the top lying nearby. And he was about to go over to it, when —

"Dave!" called a voice. "Hey, Dave, where are you?"

Then there was a rush of feet along the path outside — and there stood Chuck in the doorway, gazing about at them with the strangest expression. Silently he put his hand in his pocket and with his eyes on David's face, eyes that danced and sparkled with suppressed triumph, he slowly

— slowly — drew out his hand and — opened it. And like some marvelous rainbow-colored serpent the necklace of Ta poured from his fingers and hung there, swaying back and forth in the bright air.

There was a gasp of wonder from all those lips.

"Chuck, you found it! It's why you went back —"

"In the sand, Dave. I hunted over every inch of that beach around where we left the ship, and just when I was about to give up and go on farther, I looked down into one of those little rock pools — and I thought, 'What a beautiful crab.' And then I thought, 'But there's *never* been a crab as beautiful as that!' and I got down on my knees and put my hand in the rock pool — and pulled out Ta's necklace. It was all curled up down in there, just as neat and snug as you please, moving around every time a big wave came in from farther out and pushed a little more water into the rock pool. And Dave, pretty soon the tide would've come in again and it would have covered the necklace and —"

"— washed it away for good!" finished David, and then he went over and took the necklace in his hands as if he could not for the life of him believe that they really had it back.

Now Mrs. Topman came and put out a finger to touch the great, satiny stones — each of a different hue, cobalt, verdigris, saffron, carnelian, vermilion, emerald, ultramarine, Tyrian purple, viridian — pulsing with color so deep that you could not take your eyes from the swaying, almost living thing in David's hands. And David thought, as he moved the stones against one another, what a rich, satisfying sound they made, but he could not describe it.

Then Cap'n Tom took it in his big, red hands.

"I've traveled all over the seven seas," he said. "I've been in every corner of the world, and I've never seen anything to compare with this."

"No mere woman could wear it," said Mrs. Topman, and she took it for a moment and held it against her, then gave it hastily back to David. "No, no — it's a necklace fit only for a king."

"I wish we could have it in a big glass box," he said, "on a velvet pad in the front room of our Society. Don't you, Chuck? And there could be a sign that read 'THE NECKLACE OF TA.' But of course we can't, because it's got to be a *dead secret!*"

Chuck seemed not to understand, however.

"What society, Dave? What do you mean — ?"

Without a word, David handed Chuck Mr. Bass's last will and testament, and muttering to himself, just as David had done, his lips moving, Chuck read the whole thing through from beginning to end — then stared off at nothing over the edges of the pages as though he had been stricken and had not yet come to. Then he looked up.

"Great jumping kadiddle fish!" he exclaimed — but quietly, because by this time, what with one thing and another, he was pretty well done in.

"We've got to have a President, Chuck — remember?"

Slowly Chuck nodded, grinning, and then the two boys looked at one another and turned to Cap'n Tom.

"Would you be the President of our Society, Grandpop?"

"Chuck and I want you to be, Cap'n Tom. You're just right — you're scientific because of having charted the seas by the stars when you were young, and then having been a real topnotch navigator ever since, and because you're humorous and have imagination. We think you're exactly right!"

Cap'n Tom looked both pleased and grave.

"Boys," he said, "that's a real honor. I accept with the greatest pleasure, and I'll try always to keep my humor and imagination well to windward — that is, up where we'll stand a good chance of sailing along in a strong, steady breeze.

"And now, young fellows, I think if I might have that will, I'll just cut along over to the lawyer's and get everything settled. Annabelle, my dear, do you suppose you could drop me by?"

Mrs. Topman said she would be happy to. And even before the sound of the car had faded away around the corner of Thallᴖ Street, Chuck and David were up at the top of Mr. Bass's house.

"Numbers, Dave!" said Chuck. Tensely he waited, his fingers on the knob of the little dial on the observatory wall, ⌐hile David got out Mr. Bass's slip of paper. Solemnly David read out the combination as though it were a kind of ceremony, and smooth as velvet spun the knob, the weights clicked into place, and the safe door swung back. Inside lay the Stroboscopic Polaroid Filter, a notebook entitled *A Few Facts Concerning the Hitherto Undiscovered Satellite, Basidium-X*, another notebook entitled *Random Jottings on Some Inventions of Tyco M. Bass*, and

193

a sheet of paper on which were written rows of figures under the words "Seasonal Positions of Basidium."

Now Ta's necklace was laid away in the back of the safe, and David touched the button that caused the narrow slit to open in the dome of the observatory. Next he fitted the filter into place over the eyepiece of the telescope, and Chuck plugged in the filter cord.

"You watch first, Chuck, and I'll find the right figures and work the dials. Let's see — here's the right date." Chuck wrinkled up one eye and waited breathlessly while David muttered to himself, looking first at the paper and then, with his tongue caught between his teeth, carefully, carefully, turning the dials of Mr. Bass's telescope. Slowly it moved up and down and from left to right and back again, searching, searching.

At last the telescope was still, Chuck gazed, and then after several seconds he turned to David and without a word gave up his place. Now David, with held breath, peered into the eyepiece, adjusted it a little, then gave a low exclamation of delight.

There hung Basidium, suspended in space,

glowing unearthly beautiful in its luminous envelope of pale blue-green mist. So close it seemed, you might almost have called out to those who lived on it. Yet it was so far, thought David, that he and Chuck would never set foot on it again, never touch it again — that little world where even now Ta must be dictating to his Wise Men. David could see them in his mind, Mebe and Oru, busily writing into their Rolls of Wisdom the story, which would be handed down to their descendants, of how two strange beings had come in a creature of silver to bring them the Magic Stones from that planet which all Basidiumites call the Great Protector.

No, they might never set foot on Basidium again. Still, thought David, as long as they possessed Mr. Bass's filter, that far green world was theirs. The wonderful flight to the Mushroom Planet could be taken in the twirl of a dial and the wink of an eye, and Basidium had not been lost after all.